D0920387

LARA ADRIAN's
New York Times and #1 internationally
best-selling vampire romance novels

MIDNIGHT BREED SERIES

"Strikingly original series...delivers an abundance of nail-biting suspenseful chills, red-hot sexy thrills, an intricately built world, and realistically complicated, conflicted protagonists..."
–Booklist on Edge of Dawn (starred review)

"Riveting...If you like romance combined with heart-stopping paranormal suspense, you're going to love this book."
–BookPage on Darker After Midnight

"One of the consistently best paranormal series out there...Adrian writes compelling stories within a larger arc that is unfolding with a refreshing lack of predictability."
–Romance Novel News

"An adrenaline-fueled, sizzlingly sexy, darkly intense...addictively readable series."
–The Chicago Tribune

"Sexy, smart and compelling. A must-read series."
–Fresh Fiction

"Equal quantities of supernatural thrills and high-impact passion. One of the best vampire series on the market!"
–Romantic Times Magazine (RT Book Reviews)

NOVELS IN THE MIDNIGHT BREED SERIES
by
Lara Adrian

A Touch of Midnight (prequel novella)
Kiss of Midnight
Kiss of Crimson
Midnight Awakening
Midnight Rising
Veil of Midnight
Ashes of Midnight
Shades of Midnight
Taken by Midnight
Deeper Than Midnight
A Taste of Midnight (ebook novella)
Darker After Midnight
The Midnight Breed Series Companion
Edge of Dawn
Marked by Midnight (novella)
Crave the Night
Tempted by Midnight (novella)

...and more to come!

MARKED BY MIDNIGHT

A Midnight Breed Series Novella

☾

LARA ADRIAN

ISBN: 1939193893
ISBN-13: 978-1-939193-89-6

MARKED BY MIDNIGHT
© 2014 by Lara Adrian, LLC

Cover design © 2014 by CrocoDesigns

www.LaraAdrian.com

Available in ebook, print and unabridged
audiobook editions.

MARKED
BY
MIDNIGHT

CHAPTER 1

The night sky over London hung thick and ominous, heavy with black clouds still lingering from the evening's torrential rainstorm. The downpour had lasted for hours, driving most of the city's residents inside for shelter.

It was an advantage that Mathias Rowan and the three other Order warriors accompanying him on patrol tonight had made full use of, knowing the vampire lair they'd located in Southwark the week before was all but certain to be occupied amid the storm.

While Mathias never found it an easy thing to kill his own kind, the nest of blood-addicted Rogues squatting in the derelict brick building had to be terminated. The collection of human bones tossed in a pile in the back room of the foul-smelling lair had been more than ample justification for the Rogues' executions.

Rory Callahan, the warrior behind the passenger seat Mathias occupied in the Order's black Range Rover, let out a howl. "Damn, those were some sick, Bloodlusting fucks."

Still green and mostly stupid about life, Callahan leaned forward, grinning, the tips of his fangs still visible behind his lip, evidence of the battle rage that had gripped them all during the raid. The youngest of the squad, he hadn't seen enough death or violence yet to understand how closely every Breed male tread to the madness they'd encountered tonight.

From beside Callahan in the backseat, Deacon, the third member of the team exhaled a low, solemn curse. "They'd been killing for a while. Good thing we ashed them before they got tired of draining homeless people and moved uptown where folks were apt to notice the thinning of their herd."

Mathias grunted in grim agreement.

Only Liam Thane, the Breed warrior behind the wheel of the speeding vehicle, hadn't said a word since they'd done their business and left the lair.

Mathias had known the male for more than two decades—back when they'd both been part of a different, and since dissolved, policing organization for the Breed. Mathias had served as director in Boston then, and Thane had worked mostly covert ops around Europe and the United Kingdom.

While no one would ever call the hulking, black-haired vampire jovial, tonight Thane seemed more pensive than usual. Mathias glanced at him from the passenger seat. Thane's long hair was gathered in a tail at his nape, accentuating the severe cut of his cheekbones and stern jaw. He stared straight ahead, unblinking, focused on the rain-slicked road that followed the bank of the Thames.

"I knew one of them," he murmured, his gaze unblinking, never leaving the road. "He was a good man once...my cousin, Jacob."

The vehicle went silent at Thane's admission, nothing but the hum of the Rover's engine and the night wind buffeting the windows as it blew up off the river.

Mathias didn't offer apologies or sympathy. Thane wouldn't look for it any more than Mathias himself would. They were warriors. They had a job to do and they did it, no matter how unpleasant.

No matter how personal.

Even under ordinary circumstances, the Order's justice was swift and final when it came to dealing with the diseased killers among their race. After all, it had only been twenty years since the Breed was outed to mankind around the world in a massive Rogue attack. To say that human/Breed relations had been tenuous in the time that followed was putting it mildly.

And now, just days ago in Washington, D.C., the Order had been dealt more cause for concern. A bombing meant to disrupt a world peace summit—using a weapon powered by Breed-killing ultraviolet light—had been thwarted by the Order's founder, Lucan Thorne, with mere seconds to spare.

The attack, and the war it was meant to incite between the vampire and human populations, had been diffused, its chief architect killed, but the threat remained very real.

The Order had powerful, hidden enemies. They'd eliminated one in D.C., but they'd come away from the battle realizing there was an untold number still operating in the shadows, plotting destruction and waiting for their chance to strike again.

Compared to that, London was fortunate that aside from a Rogue problem that had just been neutralized, the only war taking place in the city was a recent spate of gang violence that had fed half a dozen bodies into the murky water of the Thames last week.

As the Rover rolled through Southwark's Bankside area, Mathias noticed a cluster of law enforcement vehicles down at the river's edge.

"Christ," he muttered. "Looks like JUSTIS is fishing another floater out of the drink."

"You want to head down there and have a look?" Thane asked.

At his nod, the big warrior turned off the road and drove toward the small gathering of human and Breed officers who served the Joint Urban Security Taskforce Initiative Squad.

They parked at the periphery of the action and walked over to the crime scene. Triangulated headlight beams pierced the darkness from the shoreline, shining out over the water where a small power boat was approaching. A pair of officers in diving gear sat at the stern, a large, unmoving object draped in a pale tarp at their feet.

Even from several yards away, Mathias's keen Breed senses allowed him to see—and smell—the dead human they had retrieved from the water.

"I'd have thought the Order's got better things to do than slum it down in Southwark."

Mathias turned his head in the direction of the booming, baritone British voice of the JUSTIS officer in charge.

Gavin Sloane was Breed, a towering, wide-shouldered male with sandy blond hair and piercing blue eyes. He came over to greet Mathias and his team with a nod and a ready grin. "If we weren't friends from way back, I might have to remind you that we got here first, so it's our party."

While the relationship between the Order and JUSTIS around the globe was guarded at best, Sloane seemed to understand, as Mathias did, the value of having allies across territory lines. They'd shared case intel from time to time over the past decade or so, and had developed a respect for each other that went beyond their jobs.

Last year, when Sloane finally conceded to settle down and take a mate, he invited Mathias to the reception that followed at the family Darkhaven. Mathias didn't know who'd been more unnerved by the presence of an Order member at the celebration—Sloane's highborn Breedmate, Katherine, or his JUSTIS officer brethren.

Sloane's broad smile didn't falter as he clapped Mathias's shoulder in greeting and glanced at the array of titanium blades and semiautomatic firearms holstered on the warriors' weapon belts from the night's raid. "Anything JUSTIS needs to be concerned about?"

"Not anymore," Mathias said. He gestured to the floater being unloaded onto the riverbank. "Anything the Order needs to be concerned about?"

Sloane shook his head. "Just another dead

scarab."

The remark referred to the tattoo each of the recent gang war victims had in common. This death brought the body count to seven. Although it wasn't unusual to find a corpse in the 213-mile river that spat them out at an impressive average of one a week, the Thames was suddenly choking on members of an unknown, but apparently lethal, new gang.

Mathias and his squad followed Sloane over to the recovery in process. Three JUSTIS officers hoisted the tarp-wrapped body onto the concrete riverbank. As the corpse settled on the ground, the plastic fell away, revealing a large human male.

"No ID on the body," Sloane said. "We'll run his prints, but it if this case follows the other six we're processing, this guy isn't likely to pop a criminal record either. Aside from the common tattoo on all of the victims, we don't have much to go on."

The dead man was dressed in dark, sodden clothing, his harsh, ugly face blanched white in death, contrasting sharply against the russet color of his full beard and shaggy red hair. On his biceps, under the short sleeves of his blood-stained T-shirt, an array of tattoos ran the length of both his beefy arms. The scarab rode the back of his right hand, the same mark and placement as on the six other murdered men.

Sloane dismissed his fellow JUSTIS officers with a curt wave as Mathias stepped closer to the corpse, studying its damage. Multiple wounds peppered the thick neck and barrel chest—deep punctures, many of them concentrated in tight clusters.

He frowned. "The other victims were pulled out of the river with bullets in their heads. This guy was stabbed with something. Repeatedly, and with a hell of a lot of force. Or passion."

"Dead is dead," Callahan murmured from beside Mathias and the rest of the team. "Maybe his killing was meant to send a stronger message than the others."

Sloane shrugged. "It's possible."

"The last body surfaced two days ago," Mathias recalled. Despite the obvious connection to the others, something didn't feel right about this victim. He looked out at the black water of the Thames, still churning from the earlier storm. The current was pulling hard in the scant moonlight, which barely penetrated the heavy cloud cover overhead. "Which way is the tide running?"

"Out," Deacon replied.

Away from London, then, toward the North Sea.

Thane's pensive glance said he was following Mathias's line of thinking too. "A couple more turns and the tide would have carried this corpse out to open water. He hasn't been in the river as long as the others had been."

"Based on the condition of the body," Sloane interjected, "we don't expect this poor bastard's been dead for even twenty-four hours." He met Mathias's gaze with one of concern. "You sensing anything out of the ordinary down here?"

His friend wasn't talking about investigator hunches or forensic evidence. Sloane was familiar with Mathias's extrasensory ability.

Every Breed vampire and every half-human Breedmate female was born with a unique ESP or telekinetic gift, some of them more useful than others. Some of those gifts were very dark, more of a curse.

Mathias's fell somewhere in the middle, though given his choice of occupation, the ability to pick up the psychic traces of violence left behind at a scene where harm was done to someone gave him an edge over most other law enforcement officials.

Still, he wasn't sure what to make of tonight's floater. "I don't feel anything unusual here, but that only means the killing didn't occur nearby."

"But you would know if it did," Sloane prompted.

Mathias nodded. "Violence leaves a psychic

mark on a place, the same way a physical blow leaves a bruise. The trick is finding it before it fades."

One of Sloane's men called to him from across the way. He raised a hand in acknowledgment, but kept his gaze trained on Mathias. Shaking his head, he blew out a chuckle. "I tell ya, Rowan, life just isn't fair. My best parlor trick is the ability to tie a decent sailor's knot without using my hands. A gift like yours, I'd have gotten promoted to JUSTIS Commissioner by now. Instead, I'm stuck bagging and tagging the city's dregs on the shit side of town."

Another vehicle rolled on to the scene, and Sloane's fellow officer shouted for him again. "About time the medical examiner showed up," he muttered. "I gotta go handle this. As for you and your team, I know I don't need to tell you that the Order's presence down here is going to make some people uncomfortable and twitchy."

Anxious looks were coming from the unit of human and Breed officers and the newly arrived coroner. Mathias grunted. "I thought uncomfortable and twitchy was standard operating procedure for you JUSTIS folks."

Sloane smirked. "You turn anything up, let me know, yeah?"

"Sure," Mathias agreed. "God knows, you need all the help you can get."

With a low laugh and a one-fingered salute, Sloane pivoted and shuffled off to join his colleagues.

"You see all the ink on this guy?" Deacon said when the warriors were alone with the body. "He's sporting some seriously hardcore tattoos."

Mathias glanced down at the elaborate artwork, cold words and cryptic symbols. The meanings of a few were easy enough to comprehend—grim indicators of kill counts and carnage, glorified, bloody depictions of violence and death.

He took out his comm unit and snapped a few quick photos of the dead man and his collection of body art.

Peering closer, Mathias noticed something interesting about one of his tattoos.

"Look at the Celtic cross on his left forearm. The six-pointed star behind it is fresh."

"And only half-finished," Thane added, staring down at the reddened skin and black ink.

Even incomplete, the star was intricate, rendered by a highly skilled hand and an artist's eye for detail.

"Hope the dumb fuck didn't pay in full for half a job," Callahan joked lamely.

None of the warriors laughed along with him. Thane and Deacon were looking at

Mathias with the same glint of possibility.

"Something's not right about this whole situation," Mathias said, thinking out loud. "Six dead members of a gang no one's ever heard of, now a seventh body turns up days later. Why?"

Callahan shrugged. "Gangs kill each other all the time. If you ask me, we should let them carry on and thank them for saving us the trouble."

The kid had a point, albeit a wrong-headed one. And dangerous besides. If a gang had ideas about bringing their war into Mathias's city, under the Order's watch, they would need to think again.

And something was nagging him about the slayings, even before this last body was pulled out of the Thames. Something he couldn't quite put his finger on yet. He needed more information. Seemed to him, the best place to begin that quest was the place where tonight's floater might have spent some of his final hours.

"Wherever he had this work started was likely one of the last places anyone saw him alive," Mathias said. "I want to find that tattoo shop. As in, tonight."

Deacon cast a skeptical look in his direction. "London is full of tattoo shops. We'll be looking for the proverbial needle in a haystack."

"We can eliminate the tourist traps and

celebrity-hound studios right off the bat," Thane said. "This guy would go to the real deal. Somewhere discreet, off the beaten path. Somewhere no one would raise an eyebrow if a thug like him walked in."

Mathias agreed. "Callahan, take the Rover back to base. Thane and Deacon, we'll cover the most ground if we split up, each of us taking the city a section at a time."

He swiveled his head upriver, against the current that would have carried the body out to sea before long. Southwark's least prosperous section of town loomed all around them, darkened buildings set against an even darker night sky.

He supposed it was as good a place to start as any.

CHAPTER 2

The buzzing drone of the tattoo machine vibrated through Nova's gloved fingertips as she inked the delicate line of a spider's web onto the left pectoral of her final client of the night.

The design was a favorite of many who came to Ozzy's studio in Southwark, men and women who'd known little else but struggles and hard times, even a long stint in prison, like the middle aged man seated in Nova's chair now.

Folks who frequented the hole-in-the-wall shop weren't going to win any humanitarian awards or keys to the city, but most of them were good people at heart.

Fancy clothes and big, sparkling mansions didn't make someone good. Nova had known that at a very young age. It had taken longer to recognize that there were plenty of good people walking around with ink all over their skin and miles of hard road in their weary eyes.

Ozzy had helped on that score.

Nova glanced over at him, puffing out her breath to blow aside the wisp of her asymmetrically cut, black-and-blue-dyed hair that had fallen into her face as she worked. The wiry, grayed and grizzled, tattooed old man who owned the shop was hunched over his latest creation, his bony, age-spotted hand as steady as a rock.

Oz had been focused on the piece for more than three hours now, the seventy-two-year-old artist working as meticulously—as reverently—as Michelangelo on the Sistine Chapel. Ozzy's canvas tonight was the masterfully designed, tattooed sleeve of an ex-con who'd lost his only grandson to cancer the weekend before last.

By hand, Oz had painstakingly reproduced the toddler's smiling face, turning the child's likeness into the tender image of a winged pixie, cavorting blissfully in the forbidding, Gothic forest that had already existed on the man's arm.

As Ozzy wiped away the running ink and blood from the final details, the shop's young apprentice took the opportunity to stop cleaning equipment and come over to have a look. Nine-year-old Eddie's freckled face lit up as he took in the finished design.

"Fuckin' righteous, Oz!" the street-wise kid exclaimed. Ozzy had taken in the former juvenile delinquent last year, much the same way he had Nova a decade ago. Eddie grinned through snaggled teeth and a scabbed lip healing over from a recent brawl at school. "Man, I cannot wait until you let me have my own chair and iron."

"And I can't wait until you clean up the storage room and swab down the toilet," Oz said, not missing a beat. "Watch the fucking cursing, while you're at it."

Ozzy was more father than boss, a role the old man had somehow slipped right into, even though he had no children or family of his own.

Like any sullen son, Eddie grumbled over the reminder of his chores. As he shuffled to the back of the shop to do as he was told, Nova paused her own work, glancing over to admire her mentor's most touching tribute.

"Beautiful work," she said, giving the old man a warm smile of approval.

Ozzy grinned with pride—a rarity—then went right back to finish cleaning and dressing the fresh ink.

Nova turned her attention back to her client, just as a dark-haired, muscular man in black fatigues walked up to the smoked glass window of the studio's entrance door.

No, not simply a man, she realized in that same instant.

A Breed male.

A vampire.

Even worse, one of the members of the Order.

He came inside, large and menacing, even without saying a word. Nova didn't startle, but the human client in her chair flinched as soon as his gaze lit on the big, heavily armed warrior.

Given the backgrounds of the majority of Ozzy's regulars, even if they'd been keeping their noses clean, none of them would be eager to cross paths with the Order's cadre of lethal peacekeepers. Nova didn't exactly welcome the intrusion either.

Before she could tell the Breed male he was obviously lost, Ozzy leveled a narrow look on the warrior from across the small studio. "Appointment only. No walk-ins. Got nothing for you, friend."

The vampire cocked his head, unfazed, in the direction of the surly greeting. Thick, wavy brown hair set off striking, pale green eyes in a face too handsome and aristocratic for his rough profession. That unnerving gaze skated over Nova, then past her, settling on Oz. "I have a few questions for you and the other artists who work here."

The accent wasn't English like hers, but American. Boston, if she had to guess. His voice was cultured and deep—as firm as the muscles she could see rippling under his fitted black combat shirt and thigh-hugging pants as he strode farther into the studio, refusing to take the hint that he wasn't welcome.

Nova's inner hackles rose in warning. She sent a glance toward Ozzy, whose challenging stare had flattened into a glare now.

"Question-asking requires an appointment too," he told the warrior. "Right now, we're booked up until sometime after hell goes glacial."

While Ozzy confronted the warrior, his client made a casual, if hasty, exit out the back door of the shop. The guy in Nova's chair seemed to want nothing more than to flee too, and likely would have if she hadn't already gone back to work on him.

Ozzy stood up, crossed his tattooed arms over his chest. "Unless you're here for ink, you got the wrong place, friend. Even then, you got the wrong place."

The warrior grunted, dark amusement in the sound. "Not very helpful."

"Helpful ain't my line of business," Ozzy growled.

"What about you?"

It took Nova a moment to realize he was

talking to her. She lifted her head and was blasted by his shrewd green gaze. Those eyes bore into her, as piercing as any needle.

She watched him take in her two-toned hair and the dozens of piercings that studded the rims and lobes of her ears. She didn't blink as his gaze moved down, over her tattooed shoulders and full-color sleeves that continued down onto her gloved hands, her extensive body art accentuated by the black leather vest she wore to work that night. It zipped up the center, showcasing even more tattoos that rode the faint swells of her breasts.

She couldn't care less what he thought of her or all of her ink and metal. She wasn't intimidated by his stare or his certain disapproval.

"What about me?" she tossed back at him irascibly, as his prolonged visual appraisal continued.

Finally, his eyes returned to hers. "I'm looking for an artist who did some specific work on someone recently. Maybe you know something about it that could help me."

He held his expression neutral, carefully so, but the dark power in his stare was unmistakable. This man, this Breed warrior, didn't have to resort to bellowing or brute force to get what he wanted.

No, he was all the more dangerous for the

way his calm demeanor coaxed her interest, her trust.

And just because he was attractive and cool-headed didn't mean there wasn't a monster lurking behind his knight-in-shining-armor good looks.

She'd gone up against worse than him and emerged unscathed.

Well, mostly unscathed.

"Nova's busy with a client, as you can see," Ozzy interjected. "She don't have time for your questions either."

Intrigue sparked in the Breed male's eyes. He was intelligent, to be sure, but at the moment, Nova read a note of suspicion in his keen gaze. "If the Order were to shut this shop down tonight, you'll both have nothing but time on your hands."

Ozzy snarled under his breath, but let the warrior continue. Without waiting for permission, the vampire took his comm unit out of the pocket of his black fatigues and flashed a photo on the device's display. "This look familiar to anyone?"

It was a close-up of a tattoo, an incomplete piece. The Celtic cross portion of it was older, a finished work, but the star behind the cross was only an outline with partial coloring applied.

"Not sure? Here's a different shot."

The warrior clicked to another photo, this

one taken slightly farther away. A wide enough angle to show the full length of a man's bare arm from below the short sleeve of a sodden, dark T-shirt to the tips of his thick fingers. Against the colorful ink and black lines of his many tattoos, the man's skin was unnaturally ashen and waxy.

Cadaver-white.

Nova's pulse kicked up a notch.

"This body was fished out of the Thames about an hour ago," the warrior confirmed. "No ID on him. JUSTIS is checking for criminal records to see if they can identify him that way, but it's doubtful they're going to find anything. All we know for certain right now is that whoever put that star on him was likely to be one of the last people to see this guy alive. If not *the* last."

Nova set down her tattoo machine and blotted the ink on her client's pec. "Let's break for a bit," she murmured to him. "Go on in back. I'll come get you in a few minutes."

"Nova." Ozzy's voice vibrated with warning.

"It's okay," she assured her overprotective boss and mentor. "I can handle this."

The Breed male was determined to have some answers, and as well-meaning as Ozzy was, his lack of cooperation was liable to get them all arrested. Or worse.

After her client had shuffled to the break

room and it was only Oz and her left to contend with their unwanted visitor out front, Nova walked over to the counter where the warrior stood. "The star is my work."

He didn't seem the least surprised to hear it, didn't even blink at the admission.

Up close, his face was even more captivating than she thought. Sharp cheekbones, strong, proud jaw line. Green eyes the color of palest sage. "Tell me what you know about the dead man, Nova."

Her name on his lips sent a shiver of awareness through her that she had to fight hard to ignore. She shrugged. "I can't tell you much, other than he was a real asshole. Came in here late last night, drunk, belligerent." An errant lock of her chin-length hair slipped from behind her ear and into her face, but she ignored it, her hands down at her sides, encased in ink-stained gloves. "As we told you, we don't take walk-ins. That goes double for intoxicated walk-ins. But this guy was insistent. No matter what we said, he wouldn't leave."

"Seems to be a pattern lately," Ozzy muttered, still glaring at the warrior.

"Like I said," Nova went on, "the guy came in late, just about the time we were closing for the night. He refused to leave without getting some fresh ink—something about com-memorating friends who'd recently passed."

Now the warrior seemed surprised. One of his brows quirked in reaction. "He had a lot of tattoos, from what I saw. I'm no expert, but seems to me he had some hardcore art on him. Death scenes. Kill counts. Some kind of affiliation mark..."

Across the studio, Ozzy cleared his throat.

"I wasn't looking at him that closely," Nova said. "I wouldn't know what other ink the guy had on his body. Even if I saw it, I'd make a point not to notice. That's what we do in this line of work, especially with the kind of clients that come through that door."

The warrior gave her a slight nod. "Why didn't you finish the tattoo?"

"I didn't have the chance. I didn't like working on him. When I told him as much, he got upset. Really upset. He stormed out in a rage, and he didn't come back."

"Son of a bitch left without paying too," Ozzy grumbled.

Those penetrating green eyes hadn't strayed from her for an instant. They studied her, made her skin feel too warm, too tight under his stare.

"Besides demanding a tattoo to memorialize his dead friends, then storming off before you could finish the work, did the victim say anything else to you, Nova?"

He did it again, spoke her name in that smooth, deep velvet voice that made her forget

23

for a second that he was not only one of the Breed, but the Order as well. A dangerous combination that she couldn't afford to get too close to, for a hundred different reasons.

"Look, I don't know what more I can tell you," she said, impatient to be done with the conversation and get back to her work. Back to her life. "I didn't spend much time talking to the guy, or looking at him. I didn't want to. I just wanted to do whatever it took to get rid of him."

"Kind of like you're doing with me?" the vampire drawled knowingly.

Nova stared at him, refusing to take his bait. Ozzy didn't give her the chance anyway.

He walked over to join her at the counter. "I got a business to run here, and Nova's got a customer waiting on her out back. Like I told you, we don't take walk-ins and we don't have time for questions. Least of all, questions about our clientele. If the Order wants to conduct some kind of investigation, I'll thank you to do it on your own turf, on your own time."

It took the warrior a moment before he acknowledged with a tight nod. "Fair enough."

He reached for a pen that lay on the counter, and jotted something down on an errant scrap of paper. He pushed the note toward Nova. "In case you change your mind and want to talk more. You can reach me anytime."

She kept her arms at her sides, her eyes steady on the shrewd gaze that seemed more suspicious than he was letting on.

Finally, the warrior turned and walked out of the shop.

Nova stood unmoving as he stepped out the door and into the night. Then she waited some more, until she was certain he was gone and wouldn't be coming back.

Only then did she reach out to retrieve the scrap that held his bold, efficient handwriting.

He'd written down a phone number and his name.

Mathias Rowan.

Nova stared at the note for a long moment.

Then she crushed the paper in her gloved fist, and dropped it into the trash bin under the counter. She had no intention of ever calling the number.

If she were lucky, she'd never run into the warrior again.

She glanced over at Ozzy, her voice quiet as she spoke. "Do you think he believed me?"

CHAPTER 3

C

*S**he lied to him.*
Mathias had known it even before he left the tattoo shop a couple of hours ago.

Hell, he'd known it almost as soon as the petite, pierced, walking, talking work of art had opened her tough little mouth.

Mathias's Breed senses had lit up about a block from Ozzy's studio, and the imprint of violence had only grown stronger the closer he got to the door.

Something bad had occurred inside that shop last night.

Something more volatile than a simple confrontation between Nova and the angry drunk later pulled out of the Thames by Gavin Sloane's unit.

Whether it was the man's actual murder or

an event leading up to it, Mathias couldn't be sure. His ability didn't translate into such neat black-and-white terms. But after talking with Nova and her surly old boss at the tattoo shop, Mathias was certain the pair were hiding something.

He meant to have the truth.

To get it, he needed to talk to Nova again— preferably without the old man there to hover over her like a snarling guard dog. It was obvious the pair's relationship went deeper than colleagues or friends, and based on the shop owner's age alone, Mathias doubted a fiery twenty-something like Nova would be sharing the man's bed.

No, it was a protective, familial kind of bond between them, not physical. Why that should stir even a small sense of satisfaction in him, he didn't want to consider.

And there was more to the young woman than met the eye too.

A lot more, Mathias was certain.

She was young, but a hard one to rattle, hard to figure out. The myriad tattoos and piercings were more intriguing to him than off-putting, giving her an unusual beauty he found hard to ignore.

There was something about her—those layers of secrets in her eyes and on her skin— that made the investigator in him curious enough to know more, even if his tastes typically ran toward more conventional-looking females. The kind who were attractive enough to be on his arm or in his bed, but easy enough to forget once his work called him back to the only true passion he'd known.

As for Nova, first and foremost, she was a person of interest in his quest to learn more about the dead man.

If he found her to be a person of interest in any other sense, he wasn't about to let that stand in the way of his duty.

The narrow, dark side alley where Mathias stood now shadowed him from view, but also gave him a clear visual path to Ozzy's shop on the other side of the main street. He'd been watching the place all this time, waiting for the opportunity to find Nova alone.

The client she'd been working on when Mathias was in the shop had exited twenty minutes earlier. The last appointment of the night would have arrived five minutes ago, except the burly dock worker had experienced a sudden change of heart mere steps away from the door and fled without bothering to cancel.

Even though humans had more or less gotten used to the idea that they shared the planet with vampires, it was still amazing what the sight of sharp fangs and glowing amber eyes could do to even the most hardass members of their population.

Mathias smirked as he pushed away from the brick wall he'd been leaning against and stepped out onto the main street.

He should call his friend in JUSTIS to clue him in on what he'd encountered earlier that night.

At the very least, he should have alerted his fellow warriors to the situation.

Instead, he approached the tattoo shop with silent purpose, prepared to do whatever it took to make Nova talk to him, confide in him about what really happened between her and the man later found stabbed and floating in the river.

Mathias needed to earn her trust if he could.

Or pull the truth out of her some other way, if her trust proved elusive.

He walked in, glad to find her alone in the shop. She had her back to him as she replenished a handful of bottles and bandages at her station. No sign of Ozzy. His station was neatly closed up, his stool pushed under his work table.

"Be right with you," Nova called over her colorful shoulder.

"Take your time. I'll wait."

She startled at the sound of his voice, but in the short moment it took for her to whirl around, she hit him with a forbidding frown. "What do you want now?"

A dozen answers sprang into his mind uninvited, none of which he was willing to speak. "I had a few more questions for you about the altercation that happened in here last night."

Her frown deepened. "I didn't say anything about an altercation."

"You didn't?"

"No. I didn't." Her English accent was cool with challenge, even if her gaze was cautious as he strode through the studio, over to her station. Mathias hadn't noticed what color her light eyes were earlier; now he stared into baby blue irises ringed with indigo. She folded her arms over her breasts. "If that's all you came to ask me, then I'm sorry you went to the trouble to come back."

He met her flat look with an easy smile. "No trouble at all." He took a seat on the client's chair in front of her.

"You can't sit there. You can't stay."

"Why not?"

Her chin hiked up a notch. "Because I'm working here. Because this is Ozzy's shop, not the Order's interrogation room."

"We don't have an interrogation room, actually. It's rare we have to resort to that. Folks tend to confess long before we feel the need to haul them in for a formal interrogation."

He was joking—pretty much. But she didn't

so much as smile. No, she was taking this all very seriously.

Deathly serious.

Mathias glanced around the empty shop. "Anyway, I don't see Ozzy now. It appears it's just you and me, Nova."

"He's here," she said. "He's upstairs in his apartment. And in case you didn't hear him the first time, we don't appreciate anyone coming in here asking questions about our work or our clients."

"I heard him. I just wonder if Ozzy's got something to hide."

"He doesn't," she replied tightly.

"Do you?"

"No."

Mathias had to give her credit. The lie slipped off her tongue without a hint of hesitation. No doubt about it, this was a woman who'd learned to keep her cards close. But had she learned it from a cold absence of conscience, or raw survival instinct?

Against all better judgment, Mathias wanted to know the answer to that—almost as much as he wanted to know why his nerve endings were tingling with the psychic aftershocks of violence.

The reading he was picking up seemed to be at its strongest right where he was sitting now.

In Nova's client chair.

She stared at him as he ran his hands over the worn black vinyl arms. Her blue eyes revealed nothing, her stance so schooled and careful, he almost began to doubt his ability to sniff out the scene of a crime.

But no, the imprint was there.

Sharp, sudden, unmistakable.

"We need to talk, Nova."

She didn't so much as flinch. "I thought we already had."

He grunted, unsure if he should be amused or infuriated by the female's apparent disregard for her own self-preservation. He hadn't tried to hide what he was. She had to know that provoking one of his kind was a bad idea.

Hell, if he wanted to, he could trance her and drag her off somewhere vastly more private than this, instead of letting her try her best to stonewall him and dodge his questions.

The idea held an unnatural appeal, especially when she stubbornly backed away, her arms still crossed as if to physically block him from pulling anything out of her. "I've got your phone number. If I have anything else to tell you, I'll be sure to let you know."

"I doubt that. I'll bet you tore up that note the minute I was gone."

She went silent, and he knew he probably hit the mark, or damn close to it.

Mathias studied her in that moment, soaking

in the full picture of her now—all of the tattoos and metal on her smooth skin, the sharp cut of her hair and the bold color that saturated the silken strands. He had no clue what her natural color might be, but found himself both fascinated and determined to have that answer and a hundred more where this female was concerned.

As for her ink, each piece of art had been beautifully, painstakingly rendered. Ozzy, he supposed, having recognized an artistry that rivaled Nova's in the old man's work on his skittish client earlier that evening.

Most of the art was abstract, beautiful vignettes of flowers and imaginative design elements. Colorful flora and fauna wrapped her lean, muscular biceps, ink covering her from the tops of her shoulders to the backs of her hands, which were tucked beneath her crossed arms.

On one of her forearms, a vine of small red roses climbed up the side of a medieval-looking wall in the vague shape of a tombstone, its rounded peak crowned with a circular window segmented by mullions and delicate tracery.

What did Nova's tattoos mean to her?

He glanced now to the design that rode just below her collarbone. Across the pert swell of her small, firm breasts, a fierce phoenix emerged from a flourish of bright flames. Its wings unfolded across Nova's chest, each feather so realistic Mathias could imagine the indomitable bird lifting up from her velvety skin to soar up to the sky, free and unstoppable.

And there was something else about the phoenix that snagged his attention now.

"What the—" Mathias had to look again to make certain of what he was seeing.

Nestled within the breast of the rising phoenix was a mark that was no tattoo at all. The small, red crescent moon and teardrop symbol was unmistakable.

A birthmark only a rare class of female bore somewhere on her body.

"You're a Breedmate."

Nova blinked, the first time he'd noticed her composure slip since he arrived. "Does it matter if I am?"

Hell yes, it mattered. To him, at least. He got up from the chair on a low curse. "You know what you are, and yet you choose to live among humans instead of the Breed?"

"That's right."

"It's a risky choice. Especially when you choose to live here, among people like the drunk who came in here last night and tried to hurt you."

"I never told you that."

Mathias held her troubled stare. "You didn't have to. I can sense something violent happened in this shop. Even if I couldn't sense

34

it, I'd know something more than what you described took place." He moved closer to her, then. Swept some of her black-and-blue hair away from her eyes when she made no move to do so. "Looking out for people who need my help is my job, Nova. I've spent the better part of my life taking monsters off the street—Breed and human alike."

She scoffed lightly and drew away from him, shoving her hands into the pockets of her black jeans. "A regular Galahad, is that it? White horse and a gleaming sword?"

He ignored her jab. She wasn't the first woman to accuse him of having a hero complex. Usually the charge accompanied the angry tears of a neglected lover who didn't want to believe him that his job, and the duty it demanded, came first. Above everything else.

With Nova, he knew her doubt in him was coming from someplace deeper. A place of real pain. A place of dark secrets that still had the power to haunt her.

"If you're in trouble, Nova, I can help you. If you'll let me."

"I don't need your help." Her reply was swift, automatic. Defensive. "I do just fine looking out for myself."

At that same moment, light footsteps sounded from a stairwell near the back of the shop. A red-haired boy came halfway down in bed-rumpled sweatpants and nothing else. His chest was scrawny, marred with old scars from abuse he must have suffered at a very young age.

"What's goin' on, Nova?" The kid's sleepy expression tensed when he saw Mathias standing in the studio. "Who's that?"

"It's okay, Eddie," Nova interjected quickly. Her voice was warm, all of her chill seeming to be reserved for Mathias. "He's just a...client. And he'll be leaving soon. Go on back to bed now. Everything's all right."

When the boy was gone, Mathias glanced at her. "Brother?"

"Close enough. Oz took him in last year when he found Eddie eating out of Dumpsters, living on the street by himself in the middle of winter. Now Eddie lives upstairs with Ozzy."

"You live with them too?" Mathias asked.

She gave a faint shake of her head, the sharp cut of her dark, two-toned hair swishing against her delicate cheek. "I have my own place on the floor above them. Ozzy rented it out to me once I turned seventeen."

"You've been with Ozzy for a while, then."

"Yeah, I have."

When she didn't volunteer anything more, Mathias studied her, looking for cracks in her tough exterior. "He seems very protective of you. Does he know about your mark—and what that makes you?"

"He knows everything about me."

"He cares for you."

She nodded. "He does. And I care for him too." She looked at him in silence for a long moment, as if debating how much of herself she needed to reveal in order to satisfy his curiosity. When she finally spoke, her voice was softer than ever. "Not that it's any of your business, but Oz is family to me. Eddie too. They're the only true family I've got."

Mathias sensed it was the most honest thing she'd told him all night.

"Look," she said abruptly, "if you want to talk, then talk. But make it quick. My last client of the night is due in any minute now." She thought for a moment, and her fine black brows furrowed. "He's late, in fact."

Mathias knew good and well the guy wasn't going to show anytime tonight. He shrugged. "So, I'll stay until he arrives."

"No, you won't," she said. "I'm still on the clock, and I've got plenty of work to do before I close up. You've got ten minutes."

"Are you this unaccommodating with all of your clients?"

She leveled an impatient look on him. "You're not my client."

"And if I was?"

She laughed. A real laugh, unrestrained and

genuine.

"Why is that funny?"

"You're hardly the type to want a tattoo."

He shrugged. "It will be my first."

"Oh, I don't doubt that," she said, her blue eyes lit with humor.

Mathias liked her eyes. He liked her laugh, and he had the fleeting awareness that he was enjoying her company more than he ought to. "What would you suggest?"

She cocked her head at him. "You don't even know what you want?"

"It doesn't matter. Surprise me."

"Surprise you?" Her pretty face scrunched up, incredulous. "It's permanent, you know."

"So, come up with something I won't regret for the next hundred years."

The ghost of a smile played along the curve of her mouth.

Damn, she had a fantastic mouth. Mathias's groin tightened as he watched her chew her lip in contemplation.

"Anything I want? Anywhere I decide to put it?"

Her choice of words only made his desire flare even hotter. "Anything. Anywhere. I'm in your hands completely."

He held her sky blue eyes, knowing full well that there were secrets in their pale depths. Dark secrets that he was still determined to uncover.

"Can I trust you, Nova?"

She stared at him for a long moment. "I guess you'll have to wait to find out. Take off your shirt."

CHAPTER 4

H ad she lost her bloody mind?

She must have, because that was the only explanation for how she'd found herself perched on her stool a couple of hours later, putting the finishing touches on a freehand tattoo she'd inked onto Mathias Rowan's back.

His powerfully muscled, utterly distracting back.

Nova hadn't wanted to notice how firm and strong he felt under her gloved fingertips. She hadn't wanted to acknowledge the warmth of his naked skin, or the beauty of his Breed *dermaglyphs*—elaborate skin markings that made all of her work pale by comparison.

She could have gone with a smaller design, placed somewhere less intimate, less time-consuming. God knew, she would have, if she'd been thinking clearly at all.

But talking with him had put an image in her head that wouldn't let go. When he took off his shirt and she saw the twin flourishes of *glyphs* on his shoulder blades, she knew she'd found the perfect placement.

And she had to admit, she took more than a little satisfaction in the thought of inking the tattoo on the persistent male's spine, instead of somewhere with fewer nerve endings just under the skin.

Given how long the work had taken, she was also thankful that she hadn't spent the whole time under his intense, unsettling gaze. Lying face-down, comfortably relaxed on the reclined work chair, made him almost seem like any other client.

Not that she'd ever had one of the Breed under her iron.

And not that any of the human clientele coming in and out of Ozzy's over the years had ever made her so keenly aware of herself as a woman the way Mathias Rowan did.

Dangerous thinking.

She had learned a long time ago how monstrous his kind could be. Even the ones you trusted the most.

Especially them, because they held the power to hurt you the deepest. To violate everything you believed in, everything you were.

To destroy you.

"Anything wrong, Nova?" Mathias's deep voice drew her out of the dark spiral of her thoughts. "You didn't fall asleep at the wheel back there, did you?"

"No. Just wrapping up."

She tried to sound casual, cool. But her throat was dry and her hands were trembling.

She didn't like to trek back to her past. It was something she deliberately avoided, wounds that had scarred over but still had the power to shred her apart if she stopped to recall them.

Just the thought of what she had endured put a knot of cold terror in her belly.

Bile burned in the back of her throat, her ears filled with the sounds of a young girl's screams.

Her screams.

"I'm almost finished," she murmured, willing the tremor out of her fingers as she placed the tattoo machine over Mathias's skin again. She completed the last of the coloring, subtle shadow and shading to bring realism to the piece.

When it was done, she blotted the design clean, then began dressing it. Mathias's Breed skin was already healing on its own, but she still stripped off her gloves and reached for ointment and bandages.

As she applied the first one, he lifted his head, bulky shoulders rising off the table. "Aren't you going to let me see it before you cover it up?"

She pushed him back down. "I thought you wanted to be surprised."

He exhaled a low chuckle. "Probably not one of my more prudent decisions, all things considered."

"It was a first." She put the last couple of bandages over the fresh ink, carefully patting them into place. "If you ask me, only an idiot or a lunatic would let an unknown artist go freestyle on them for two full hours."

He grunted. "So, which one do you think I am?"

Nova smiled in spite of herself. "I haven't decided yet."

"Maybe I'm just an excellent judge of character." With that, he rose all the way up and pivoted around to a seated position on the edge of the chair.

Good lord, it was distracting to watch him move. He was muscular and long-limbed, powerful arms and thick shoulders framing a sculpted chest and ripped abdomen.

Mathias leaned forward slightly, elbows braced on his knees. The look he gave her sent her pulse skittering in her veins. "Maybe we both need to trust each other a little bit here, Nova. What do you say?"

Those penetrating eyes she had avoided all the while she was working on him now bore into her with the intensity of twin lasers.

Heat seared her, and she couldn't dismiss it as anything other than what it was.

Curiosity.

Awareness.

Desire.

How long since she'd felt any of that? God, had she ever—*really ever*—felt such an immediate, undeniable pull toward a man?

She didn't dare let it take hold of her now.

Not with him.

It would be a mistake she couldn't undo.

Letting herself get close to one of the warriors from the Order—particularly one whose investigation had brought him to her doorstep in the first place—was a mistake she refused to make.

Pivoting away from him, she began cleaning up her station. "You'll want to remove the bandages after a couple of hours. I can give you some ointment to use for the next few days, but the way your kind heals, I doubt you'll need it."

"My kind," he murmured from behind her.

She shot him an arch glance over her shoulder. "I don't suppose I have to remind you to stay out of the sun."

He was staring at her, and he didn't look pleased. "You're dismissing me. Always so eager to get rid of me. I have to wonder why that is."

She shrugged. "You asked for a tattoo and I gave you one. So, unless there's anything else—"

"There is, Nova." He held her in a piercing, narrowed stare. "What are you afraid I'm going to find out? You and I both know the man who came in here last night didn't leave the way you explained it to me."

Anxious now, she pushed her hands into her pockets and faced the Breed warrior. "If you want to accuse me of something, do it."

He exhaled a sharp breath. "I'm not ready to say you had something to do with his death, but I know you're not telling me the truth. What do you know about the others?"

Confusion bled into her dread. "What others?"

"The six other men pulled out of the Thames in the past week, Nova."

"I have no idea what you're talking about." And she didn't. But he wasn't baiting her, that much she knew, just from the unflinching seriousness of his expression. "Why would you think I know anything about anyone else?"

"Because all of the men—including the one who came here last night—had a similar mark on the backs of their right hands." He took out his comm unit and brought a photo up on the display. "This tattoo, Nova."

She didn't want to look, but there was no avoiding it. Glancing down, she saw the heavy black shape of a tattoo she recognized instantly. "It looks like a beetle. A scarab."

"Yes," Mathias said grimly. "Ever seen it before?"

She shook her head, preferring his suspicious gaze over the sight of the dead man's washed-out skin and its ugly mark. "I told you earlier tonight, in my line of work, it's best not to pay too close attention to what people have on them."

He made a dubious sound in the back of his throat. "I know what you told me. I also know there were six unidentified bodies chilling in the morgue with bullets in their heads before we pulled up their friend tonight. If you can shed some light on where they came from, or who they are—"

"I can't," she blurted.

Too fast, because his shrewd gaze went a bit colder then.

"I trusted you tonight, Nova," he said after her silence stretched out between them. "I want you to know that you can trust me too."

She scoffed and went back to straightening her station. "Is that what this was about—some kind of exercise to win my trust? You don't have enough time or skin for that, vampire."

He moved so fast, she wasn't even aware he was on his feet before his strong hands took hold of her shoulders.

Gently—so tenderly, it shocked her—he turned her around to face him. His pale green eyes flashed with sparks of amber as his temper spiked. "If I wanted to force you into coming clean with me about anything, I have far more effective methods than letting you scrape me with needles and ink for the past two hours."

She let her chin lift, defiance surging through her, almost as powerful as the sheer panic that gripped her at his threat.

But he'd never see her fear.

She'd give that to no one ever again. "I'm not afraid of anything you can do to me. Believe me, it's already been done."

She'd run too far, worked too hard to start over. She'd left all of the pain and horror behind her, refusing to let the demons she'd barely escaped ever have the chance to catch up to her again.

But they had.

They'd caught up to her last night, when a drunken thug wandered into the shop and threatened to tear open the vault of awful secrets she'd carried inside her for most of her life.

And she had to remember that someone like Mathias Rowan could smash that door open in ways no other man could. For all she knew, he could be playing her now, trying to make her trust him only so he could betray her when it served him.

If he found out the truth, he could send her back to that place. Back to the monster who had taken so much from her—everything, in fact.

Nova would die before she let herself fall back into her tormentor's hands.

She would kill before she let that happen.

The body retrieved from the river last night was proof enough of that.

"Christ," Mathias murmured softly, as if sensing the burden she carried. "Who was it that hurt you? Tell me, and I'll make them pay."

He reached out to her, his blunt fingertips lightly grazing her cheek. She pulled away at once. "I think you should leave now, Mathias."

He didn't speak for a long moment. Didn't move.

Then he blew out a rough curse. "Yes, it will be for the best if I go now."

He moved away from her and put his shirt back on. As he dressed, Nova walked to the shop's front door and opened it.

If he didn't leave soon, she wasn't sure she could trust herself to let him go.

He crossed the room, pausing in front of her. His sensual mouth was tense, amber light still glowing in irises.

He wanted her, possibly as much as he wanted the truth.

The knowledge should have terrified her. Instead it left her heart pounding frantically in her breast, all the air in the room charged with a current of anticipation.

A current of heated understanding.

When Mathias spoke, his deep voice was thick, little more than a growl of sound. "What do I owe you for your work?"

"Nothing." She shook her head, forcing herself to hold his knowing gaze. "I don't want anything from you."

For the longest time, he just stood there, measuring her. Looking right through her.

God help her if he ever saw the truth.

"When you're ready, I want you to tell me what happened here, Nova. All of it. As for the rest..." His deep voice trailed off, and he gave a weary shake of his head. "You know how to reach me."

She stepped away from the open door. "Good-bye, Mathias."

He walked out.

As soon as he had, she closed the door behind him and threw the bolt.

Then she sagged back against the battered

black steel and released the shaky breath that had been burning in her lungs.

CHAPTER 5

ꙮ

At barely five a.m. the next morning, Nova stood outside the green doors of the Southwark coroner's office employee entrance in a baggy gray sweatshirt and jeans, her hair concealed under a knit cap. She rapped twice, her breath steaming as she waited in the pre-dawn chill.

The door creaked open, revealing a reed-thin man in a white lab coat. His graying, dishwater blond hair was caught up in an elasticized plastic cap, baring his neck and the edges of the extensive tattoos that weren't quite concealed by the collar of his coat.

"Thanks for doing this, Stan."

"No worries," her long-time client said. "I'm the only one on shift right now, so come on in."

She'd called him last night, immediately after Mathias Rowan left the shop. Stan hadn't asked any questions about why she was interested in the recent arrivals at the area morgue. That she wanted to come down and have a look had been explanation enough for one of Ozzy's regulars.

Even better, Stan wasn't going to require her to present ID and sign in, the way she'd have to if her visit had been anything but covert.

"This way," he said, leading her inside to a cold room of white tile and stainless steel. The place reeked of antiseptic and death. "All of the John Does are in those coolers on the far wall, Nova. Take as much time as you need."

She gave him a nod, then waited until she was alone in the room.

She walked over to one of the latched cabinet compartments and opened it. The drawer clicked as she pulled it out, the only sound in the place, now that it was just her and the dead.

The body on the refrigerated stainless steel slab emerged feet-first, a toe tag proclaiming him *Unidentified Caucasian Male*. Nova tugged the drawer out the rest of the way, and in moments she was looking over the face of the thug from the other night at Ozzy's.

Orin Doyle.

The name tasted like acid to her senses, the memory of his ugly sneer and terrifying threats chilling her even more than the cold air in the morgue.

She wasn't interested in him now. He wasn't the reason she hadn't been able to sleep last night. He wasn't the reason she had come to the coroner's office on an investigative mission of her own.

She had to know more about the others.

Why were men with scarab tattoos suddenly turning up in London?

Had they known she was there?

Doyle had stumbled upon her by accident, but what if there were others in the city now too? Others who might come looking for her, if they weren't already...

Nova had a thousand questions, but there was only one she could resolve here.

It was someplace to start, at least. If she were lucky, she might learn if her secret was safe, or if she needed to run again.

She could hardly bear the thought of leaving Ozzy after all he'd done for her. The old man had been her only family for almost half her life now. And Eddie, the kid brother she never had.

Her heart hurt to remember another brother, one she knew a long time ago. Older than her by a lifetime, it seemed, Aedan had been the sole kindness in a beautiful, glittering house full of hideous, private brutality and unspeakable abuse.

A Breed male born to the monster who'd adopted Nova when she was a young child, Aedan never knew what she'd been going through. She'd been forced to smile and act her part, keep all of her toxic secrets bottled up inside.

And then Aedan left their Darkhaven home, never to return, and from then on she'd been truly alone.

Ozzy and Eddie were the family she made for herself in the time since, and after last night, she'd dragged Oz into the violence and ugliness of her past too.

Not that he hadn't known the worst of it before then.

She looked down at the tattoos he'd skillfully made on the backs of her hands when she turned seventeen. She'd begged him for the ink—her first—and he'd reluctantly agreed only because he understood what it meant to her.

The mark on the back of her right hand, the tattoo she'd pleaded with Oz to conceal, was barely visible anymore, obscured by his beautiful art.

Nova rubbed her thumb over the exotic Egyptian eye and artful flourishes that had once been an entirely different image—one she hated with every fiber of her being.

A black scarab, identical to the one on Orin Doyle's right hand.

The ones she knew she was going to find on the hands of the other dead men in this room.

Nova shoved Doyle's body back into its cabinet and closed the door. She opened the compartment next to him and pulled out the drawer. The man's face was unfamiliar, but he had the scarab mark on his hand, just as Mathias had told her.

Nova opened two more coolers and found two more scarab tattoos. All of the thugs had been in service to her adoptive father.

She shook off a chill that went deep into her marrow. She didn't want to know more, but she couldn't stop now. For her own safety, she had to understand what was going on.

And for that, she would have to call upon the dark ability she'd been born with as a Breedmate.

Steadying herself for what was to come, she reached out with her right hand and took hold of the waxy fingers of the dead man closest to her.

A jolt of memory hit her the instant she touched him.

Not her memory, but his.

The awful talent she despised had lost none of its power. It rose up swiftly, vividly, giving her a crystal-clear picture of the dead man's final moments.

Images flooded her mind as if she was living them herself: she saw the dark water of the Thames under a night sky, a large steel shipping container being unloaded onto a dock.

Someone spoke to her—to the man who would be dead before long—Russian words she couldn't comprehend. More men stood nearby, speaking urgently, making some kind of deal, from what she could discern from their body language and gestures.

Then the sharp report of gunshots nearby.

Anxious shouts went up, and Nova's line of vision swung around abruptly as the man whose gaze she was seeing through suddenly turned his head. Orin Doyle stood there, a pistol raised at forehead level in front of Nova's eyes.

Doyle grinned, then fired.

Nova's connection cut short as the man dropped to the ground, shot dead at point-blank range by someone he knew and trusted.

"What the hell?"

Sick from the power of her gift and what it showed her, she let go and moved to another of the bodies to repeat the process. Doyle had killed him too, another shot ringing out elsewhere at the same time, dropping one of the Russians just before Nova's connection to Doyle's victim severed.

She moaned, unable to continue.

Using her ability always left her nauseated and weak. After so many years away from it, and after the grisly visions she'd just witnessed, it was all Nova could do to return all of the dead back to their coolers and close everything up.

She staggered into a vacant restroom down the hallway, her head pounding ferociously, stomach rebelling with each step.

She hit the first stall and retched into the toilet.

As she slumped against the cold metal wall, her mind spun with even more questions than when she'd first arrived at the morgue.

What were Doyle and the other men up to at that dock?

Why had he turned on his own?

And most troubling of all, how could Nova answer any of her questions without risking herself and everyone she cared for?

~ ~ ~

Fresh out of the shower, Mathias pivoted his head over his shoulder to get another look in the mirror at Nova's handiwork on his back.

A sword, for fuck's sake.

A gleaming, perfectly rendered, realistic-looking blade that extended tip-down along the length of his spine.

The kind of sword a knight would carry.

Mathias chuckled wryly to himself. She'd called him Galahad, after all. Apparently the joke was on him—literally.

Whatever her intent, he actually liked the tattoo.

He like her too, and that was a fact that had been eating him up ever since he'd returned to Order headquarters the night before.

His interest in her was a problem he didn't want to acknowledge, but it was rather hard to deny the way she'd stirred his interest last night. Feeling her warmth leaning over him for two hours while she worked on him had been torture.

Her gloved hands all over his naked back, sure and steady, as she'd created a work of art on his skin had made him long to feel her touch in other places.

The subtle, fleeting graze of her lovely little breasts, so precariously contained within the zippered black leather vest she seemed to think passed for clothing, had given him a hard-on he had barely managed to rein in.

He'd wanted to kiss her, and no doubt would have, if she'd been anything but prickly and evasive with him. He might have done more than kiss her, had she not been the wiser of them and all but tossed him out on his ass and slammed the door behind him.

So, instead, he'd gone back to base with an uncharacteristically bad attitude and a need to be left alone to lick his damaged male pride and reassure himself that fiery, enigmatic Nova was a problem he damned well didn't need.

He was still trying to convince himself of that today. Not a good potential, considering it was going on sundown and just the thought of her had his cock rising to attention all over again.

What would his old friends back in Boston tell him to do about Nova?

He had half a mind to call and find out.

Then again, he could predict most of their reactions without consultation.

Leave the female alone.

Mind on duty, not your dick.

Find another distraction—one that wasn't a person of interest in a homicide.

Of course, there were no less than ten of the most seasoned Order members who wouldn't have been able to follow their own sage advice. Mated warriors, each with their own blood-bonded Breedmate that they loved more than life itself. Some of the Order had even fathered children in the twenty years Mathias had known them.

All things he'd never aspired to, never paused long enough to consider he might want.

Not that he wanted any of that now.

And certainly not with a difficult, secretive woman like Nova.

What kind of name was that, anyway?

Who was her family?

She'd been living with Ozzy at least since she was seventeen, according to what little she'd divulged. Mathias guessed she'd been under the old man's wing for longer than that. He just didn't know the how or why of it.

Just as he didn't know who had been responsible for the hurt she'd shown him—however briefly—when she'd admitted to him that nothing could be done to her that she hadn't already endured.

Who the fuck had wounded her so deeply?

Christ, every time he thought about her, it raised new questions. Stirred more curiosity in him to peel back the endless layers of secrets and camouflage she seemed to hide behind.

Mathias didn't want to think about what he would need to do if peeling back any of those layers proved her guilt in the killing of the man who confronted her in Ozzy's shop.

He would be duty-bound to surrender her to JUSTIS and let the system decide her fate.

Somehow, he didn't think she'd stand by and wait for that to happen.

Nova's headstrong, defiant gaze in the shop last night had told him that much. No, she would run before she'd let herself be shackled.

But would she do anything more desperate?

Mathias dreaded being the one to find out.

His head was still churning on that troubling scenario when his comm unit buzzed with an incoming call. He grabbed it off the counter, recognizing his friend Gavin Sloane's number.

"Don't tell me you fished another scarab out of the Thames," he murmured by way of greeting.

"No," Sloane said. "But we may have a lead on the seven on ice down at the morgue."

Mathias's senses went taut with attention. "How so?"

"They had a visitor early this morning. Coroner's got surveillance video of a woman being admitted into the morgue by one of the graveyard shift employees. She seemed to know at least a few of the victims, held their hands for a couple of minutes before rushing out of the room like she was going to lose her shit."

The blood in Mathias's veins started hammering hard with warning. He'd told Nova about the bodies in the morgue. She had seemed shocked, even troubled. But could she have known those men? Could she be mixed up in not just one slaying, but all seven of them?

Ah, fuck. Everything Mathias stood for demanded that he voice his suspicions to his friend, here and now. Yet there was a part of him that wanted to shield Nova from that kind of trouble.

He wanted to be certain before he tossed her into the fray.

"Do you have a description of this woman?" he asked, his voice sounding wooden, even to his own ears.

"It's not great footage to work with, unfortunately," Sloane said. "She was wearing a hat and baggy clothing, no doubt to conceal her appearance."

Mathias gripped his comm like a life line, despising himself for the relief that coursed through him. "Damn, that's too bad. It might've been helpful to find this woman and bring her in for questioning, see if she can give us any IDs on the dead."

Sloane chuckled. "We'll find her. The employee who let her in isn't cooperating, but we saw the woman's hands on the feed. She's got tats all over her. Won't take long to ID the bitch just based on the markings we recovered from the video. Already got some of my men working on that. I'll be joining up with them as soon as the sun sets. You and your team care to lend a hand on this tonight?"

"Can't," he blurted. "We've got a...got a lead on another Rogue's nest down in Lambeth that bears looking into. Once my squad wraps up, I can send them your way."

"Nah, don't worry about it. We've got this

one covered." Sloane chuckled. "I can think of worse things than conducting body scans of the females working the area tattoo shops. You go have fun with your Rogue hunt. I'll be in touch if we shake anything loose tonight."

Sloane hung up, and Mathias stood there for a long moment, staring at the reflection of his scowling face in the mirror.

The face of a man who had just lied to an old friend, and who was about to defy his pledge to the Order by sending his team of warriors on a wild goose chase down in Lambeth, if only to give Mathias time enough to warn Nova that whatever her secrets were, they were about to catch up with her.

CHAPTER 6

He wasted no time in seeking her out.

With mission directives given to his team to flush out a warehouse he knew would yield nothing, Mathias himself took off for Southwark the moment the sun dipped below the horizon.

When his street side surveillance of Ozzy's shop showed Nova's absence in the studio that evening, Mathias took a chance that he might find her in the apartment she lived in on the third floor.

He entered through the back of the old brick building, mentally flipping the lock with an ease all of the Breed possessed. A rear stairwell climbed up from the ground level. Mathias ascended to the top in the time it would take a mortal to blink.

Once he was standing in front of what had to be Nova's apartment, he cooled his heels and let his knuckles fall against the unmarked door. He heard faint movement inside, bare feet padding over hardwood floors.

Nova's voice sounded weary on the other side of the wood panel as she freed the deadbolt. "Eddie, you were just up here five minutes ago. Now, I told you, I'm not feeling well tonight, so, please, just let me—"

Her words cut short the instant she opened the door and saw Mathias standing there. What little color she had in her face in that moment drained away. She was dressed for a quiet night in, loose-fitting black sweats and a strappy black tank. Mathias didn't know what was more appealing—her perky breasts zipped into last night's tight black leather vest, or braless beneath the scrap of cotton that was all to prevent him now from taking them into his hands.

He cleared his throat, but couldn't quite mask the emerging presence of his fangs. "I hope you don't mind if I come in."

Her chin hiked up. "Yes, actually, I bloody well do mi—*hey!*"

He stepped forward, taking hold of her upper arms as he strode inside. He steered her into the living area and closed the door behind him with a stern mental command.

When the deadbolt clicked back into place, Nova's indigo-ringed, light blue eyes went from shock to outrage. "What the hell do you think you're doing?"

"That's what I came to ask you," he growled back at her. "Where were you this morning?"

She glared, but there was a guilty glint in her gaze. "I don't answer to you."

"Tonight you do, Nova. If you're smart—and I know you are—you'll tell me everything now. What happened the other night in Ozzy's shop, why you went to the morgue this morning and why...all of it."

She swallowed hard. "I don't know what you're talking about."

"Damn it, woman. Don't lie to me. I'm not your enemy."

"Yet," she finished quietly. "I don't even know you."

He swore roundly. "Yes, you do, Nova. Do you think if I wanted to hurt you, or if I didn't care what happens to you, I'd be standing here right now, asking you to trust me?"

"Why?" Her voice was so thin, he hardly heard it over the drumming of his pulse.

"Why, what?"

"Why do you care, Mathias?"

For a moment, he wasn't sure how to answer that. He couldn't point to any one reason that made sense to him, and yet there were a hundred things about this damaged, but resilient, woman that he wanted to understand. He only wanted her to give him that chance.

"I care, because I see a beautiful, strong young woman who's hurting—badly—and I want to take some of that hurt away, if I can. I see a scared little girl behind all of your ink and metal and claws, and I want her to know that she can be safe."

Tenderness shone in the soft blue of her eyes. Her answering scoff, however, was bitter. "I don't need some goddamned white knight riding to my rescue, Mathias. I thought we already covered that."

"Yeah, we did," he said. "And now I've got the tattoo to prove it."

She dipped her head, not quite in time to hide the sudden, slight curve of her lips. "I suppose you hate it."

"Not at all." He lifted her chin on the tips of his fingers. "If you didn't want me playing gallant knight to your obstinate lady, then you shouldn't have put Sir Galahad's sword on my back."

He expected her to smile, maybe even laugh. But instead a pained look crossed her lovely face. "I can't do this."

She reached up to draw his hand away from her, and that's when he saw—really saw—the colorful design that covered the back of her right hand. The blue eye surrounded by elaborate swirls and flourishes had looked like some kind of hex symbol to him on first glance. Now, he saw something else hidden within the mark.

"Jesus Christ." He grabbed her wrist to hold her steady while he took a closer look. "You have the same mark as the dead men. I can see the scarab. Holy fuck, you tried to bury it under this other design, but it's there."

Fury and confusion sparked in him like a match struck against dry tinder. Mathias felt his gaze heat as the amber light of his anger ignited in the green of his irises. "Are you one of them, Nova?"

She shook her head. "No."

"Did you kill them?"

"God, no!" She moaned then, a terrified sound. The sound of an animal caught in a snare. "Mathias, please..."

He held fast to her wrist, refusing to let her evade him now. "There is video of you at the coroner's office this morning, Nova. After I told you about the dead men with scarab tattoos, you went to the morgue to see them. You touched them, held their hands. Do you know who they were, or where they came from? Were you mourning any of them?"

"No," she answered thickly. She struggled against his grasp, but he didn't release her.

Right now, he needed the answer to that last question more than any of the others. "It was nothing like that."

"Then what was it like? Tell me, Nova. Talk to me. I'm not the only one who's going to make you explain what you've done."

When she looked up at him in question, in panic, he said, "The video was shown to JUSTIS officers today. They haven't identified you yet. Since the employee who let you inside isn't talking, I assume he's a friend. All he's done is delay law enforcement from finding you. But they will, and you'll not only have to answer for the killing I'm certain happened here in the shop, but the other victims you seem to have some connection to as well."

Her breath leaked out of her, taking some of her fight along with it. "I didn't kill the man who came in here last night. I wanted to. But he was stronger than me. He clamped his hand around mine and he made...threats. Then he grabbed my hair with his other hand. He wouldn't let go." She exhaled a heavy sigh. "Ozzy only wanted to protect me. He did what anyone would do, what I couldn't do at that moment. After he was dead, Oz and I dumped the body in the river. We tried to weight it down, but there was a storm overnight..."

Mathias listened to her in silence, watched her confess an account he hadn't quite guessed on his own. And there was a detail that still troubled him. "You said the man made threats. What kind of threats, Nova?" When she didn't answer after a moment, he freed her hand in order to brush his fingers along the taut line of her jaw. "You knew him, didn't you."

She nodded once. "From...before. I hadn't seen him in ten years, but I would've recognized him anywhere. I tried to pretend I didn't—that's why I started to give him the tattoo he demanded. But then, after I started working on him, he recognized me too, even though I look very different now. I *am* very different now."

"Was he the one who hurt you...before?"

"One of them," she said. "His name was Orin Doyle."

Mathias would dig into that name the first chance he got. He only wished he had the opportunity to deliver some pain to the bastard personally before Ozzy stabbed him. "And the others in the morgue?"

Nova shook her head. "I didn't know them at all. They were associates of Doyle's, but he betrayed them. He executed them in cold blood down on a dock at the river. There were others with them. They were speaking Russian, I think, making some sort of deal with Doyle's men. But it all seemed to go wrong. At least one of them was shot too, killed, but not by Doyle."

Mathias scowled, skeptical. "How can you know all of this?"

"Because that's what I saw when I touched the bodies. I saw the last few minutes of their lives. I saw how they died. I saw who did it."

At first, he wasn't sure what she was saying, then realization dawned. "Your Breedmate gift is a dark one. It can't be easy for you, having that kind of ability."

She shrugged, but her voice was quiet, haunted. "I don't think about it. I don't use it. Not unless I have to."

He nodded, solemn with understanding. For all the times he cursed his own grim ability, it was nothing compared to what Nova must experience when she called upon hers. And yet she bore her burden—all of them—with stalwart courage. An extraordinary woman, in so many ways.

As for what she'd revealed just now, Mathias had suspected some kind of massacre, but the news of Russians being part of whatever went down was valuable intel the Order and JUSTIS didn't have. Still, it only raised more questions.

"Do you know what brought Doyle and those other men to London? You said it seemed like some kind of deal was taking place," he said, trying to put the pieces together. "Do you know what that deal was about? Do you know why the killings happened?"

"No. That's not something I could detect with my gift." She met his gaze solemnly. "I don't know any of those answers, I swear to you."

"And the scarab, Nova?"

"What about it?"

"What does the mark mean? There's no gang known to law enforcement that uses that symbol, so who does it belong to?"

She shook her head mutely, pivoting from him to pace a few steps away. "It's not a gang. It's a family symbol. My family."

He walked up behind her. Gently rested his palms on her shoulders. "Tell me their name, Nova."

"Now, you ask too much," she murmured. "I ran away from them a long time ago, for good reason. I won't speak the name and let that evil touch me again."

Mathias wanted to press the issue, persuade her to give up the rest of her secrets. But she was trembling under his light touch. The tough-talking, hard-looking woman was shaking like a fragile leaf.

He coaxed her around to face him. "It's okay. We'll figure it out."

"I'd like to believe that," she whispered. "But I just don't see how."

Mathias brushed his thumb over her lips,

silencing her worries. For now, at least—for a moment—he didn't want her to be afraid. She stared up into his eyes, and he knew there was nothing he wouldn't do to keep this woman safe.

"We'll figure it out," he told her again, softer this time.

Then he bent his head down to hers and kissed her.

She didn't resist him, didn't push him away with defensive words or protesting hands. No, she wrapped her arms around him as he drew her deeper into his embrace. She kissed him back, with the same heat and need that was coursing through his own veins.

Mathias stroked his hand up the inked sleeve of her arm, then caught her nape in his palm while his tongue tested the giving seam of her lips. She parted for him, took him in on a quiet gasp.

He didn't know how he'd managed to let the moment go from one of confrontation and mistrust to one of fierce, undeniable desire.

The comfort he'd meant to offer had incinerated, melted into something powerful. Something he wasn't noble enough to resist.

He only knew that he wanted her.

And if he didn't find the will to put the brakes on soon, there would be no turning back.

~ ~ ~

She wanted to push him away.

She wanted to tear her mouth from his, retreat to the other side of the room, out of his arms.

She wanted to scream, but it wasn't terror or panic making her senses explode with the need to escape. It was desire.

Raw, hungry, impossible desire.

Something she had never known, had never expected to feel so powerfully. She could hardly contain it, the need Mathias's kiss stirred inside her.

She could hardly breathe, hardly think straight, for the way it coiled around her, stripping away her defenses. Removing each carefully placed brick in the wall she'd built around herself ages ago.

If she let it fall, there would be no building those defensive walls again—not with him.

She would be at Mathias's mercy, and he already knew too much.

He'd seen too much.

Nova moaned, forcing herself to break away from the pleasure of his kiss.

"Mathias, I don't...I can't," she stammered, not even sure what she was trying to deny anymore. She only knew that if she let him continue touching her, kissing her, wanting her, she would be lost to him completely. "Don't do this to me."

"Don't do what?" His deep voice was a growl against her cheek, then down along the side of her neck. "Don't kiss you? Don't want you? What shouldn't I do, Nova?"

"Everything." She drew back from him then, crossing her arms over herself when his body heat was gone and a chill settled into her bones. She put more distance between them, needing it in order to convince herself that she could do this—that she could push him away when it was the last thing she wanted in that moment. "I'm scared, Mathias."

He took a step toward her. "Don't be. Not of me."

She bit her lip, trying to conjure the words she needed to save herself from giving in to him, from falling any further. But her heart wouldn't cooperate with her head. Words lodged in her throat.

Then a knock on the door did the hard work for her. Eddie's voice sounded on the other side. "Nova, you there? Let me in, will ya?"

God, she couldn't let the kid see that she had someone in her apartment. Especially not a Breed male, whose glowing amber eyes and sharp white fangs were liable to send Eddie screaming back to Ozzy downstairs in the studio.

She'd begged off her shift tonight and cancelled all of her appointments, claiming she was sick. That lie would hurt even worse, if they knew she was up there thinking about getting naked with Mathias.

Which she wasn't, she told herself. Not thinking about it, or doing it.

She closed her eyes, exhaling a heavy sigh. "Another time, Eddie, okay?"

"Oz sent me to check on you, make sure you're not pukin' your guts out or something."

"I'm not," she said, casting Mathias a pointed look. "I'll be fine, I promise. I just need some time alone, that's all. Tell Oz not to worry about me."

"Sure, but you know he's gonna worry 'til he sees you for himself. He says you've never called in sick once, Nova."

"I'll come down later, promise."

"All right, then," he agreed after a moment. "I'll let him know."

When Eddie's footsteps faded into silence, Nova released a pent-up breath. "I can't do this. You should leave, Mathias."

He moved in closer. "I don't want to leave."

"You heard Eddie. He and Oz are worried about me. They're going to wonder what I'm doing up here." She dropped her gaze to avoid Mathias's smoldering eyes. "We need to stop this now. You need to leave, and I should go—"

"You don't want to go." He guided her face back to him, refusing to let her hide. His irises blazed bright with amber light, pupils so thin they were almost swallowed by the heat of his desire. The tips of his fangs gleamed behind the sensual line of his lip as he spoke. "You don't want to stop what's happening between us. You can't deny it, Nova. No more than I can."

She stared up at him, miserable with need. She saw that same need written in the intensity of his gaze, in the iron firmness of his square jaw as he parted his lips and descended on her once more.

He claimed her mouth this time, and she sank into it willingly, wantonly.

His kiss was both tender and hungry now, coaxing and demanding. Her tongue found his and he moaned, a low, tormented sound.

He tasted so good. Hot and powerful, primal. Yet his arms were protective, careful as they wrapped around her and held her close.

Nova leaned into his strength, into the warmth he offered within the circle of his arms.

She should be afraid. All of her old defenses fired like warning shots, cautioning her that this passion was a dangerous thing. He was a dangerous man—the worst kind, a Breed male, like the one who had violated her so brutally long ago.

But her instincts soothed under Mathias's touch. Her fears had no place here, when he was kissing her, caressing her, stoking a need in her that she had never known.

He had asked her to give him her trust. Where Nova clung to it so tightly when it came to her past and the life she left behind, now, sheltered in Mathias's arms, under the gentling power of his intoxicating kiss, she knew only surrender.

She had no fight in her as he dragged her deeper into his embrace, pressing his body to hers. His arousal was obvious, thick and hard at her abdomen. He groaned as he moved against her, tension rippling through him like a current.

"Do you want this, Nova?" he murmured against her mouth. His voice was gravel, a rough, hot growl that should have sent panic into her veins, but instead kindled a higher flame in her core. "Tell me. I need to know if you're feeling this too."

She had a thousand reasons to deny it, to deny him.

A thousand reasons to push him away and hope she never saw him again.

But when she parted her lips, only one word slipped off her tongue. "Yes."

CHAPTER 7

He hadn't truly expected that answer.

But that didn't keep Mathias from taking Nova's petite frame up in his arms, then carrying her through the small apartment to the bedroom at the end of the short hallway.

He knew she wanted him. Hell, he knew she was as fevered and hungry with desire as he was. He tasted it in her kiss. He saw it in her pale blue eyes, which had gone dusky with need before he'd even brushed his mouth against hers the first time.

But he'd fully anticipated her rejection, not a breathless surrender.

She was scared to be with him; she'd admitted that easily enough.

What she hadn't been so forthright about

was the reason for her fear. Part of him wanted to believe it was because she was inexperienced with sex, but the few things she'd told him about her past had given him reason enough to understand that Nova wasn't a virgin.

She'd been misused before, and it made him want to gather her to him like a broken bird and soothe her with gentling words and careful hands.

But Nova was also a fiery woman—a sexy, vibrant female who made everything male in him want to stand up and beat his chest, show her in the most carnal, primal way that she was his tonight, and that no man would ever come near her again without coming through him first.

As he walked over to the bed and sat her down on the edge of it, Mathias struggled with the two warring sides of himself.

The urge to get her naked beneath him had his blood running hot in his veins, his fangs throbbing as fiercely as the erection that strained against his pants, demanding release.

It took all the control he had not to act on that impulse. Instead, he smoothed his hand over her silky black-and-blue hair, let it sift between his fingers. He stroked her creamy, velvet-soft cheek, let his thumb trace the shell of her ear, over the combination of small silver and black hoops that rode its delicate perimeter.

He caressed the satiny lengths of her tattooed arms, committing every colorful inch to memory as both his fingers and his admiring gaze traveled her skin. He studied the Gothic-looking design on her left forearm—the one he'd initially dismissed as a tombstone. On closer look now, he realized he'd seen the image somewhere in the city. Had walked by it a thousand times on his regular patrols of Southwark, in fact.

"It's the rose window on the remains of the old Winchester Palace, down by Southwark Cathedral," Nova said, when he stroked the tattoo in silent contemplation. "That's where I met Ozzy, after I first came to London. The Cathedral only gives homeless people shelter for the night, so I hung out at the ruins during the day, sketching to pass time. Oz was there one afternoon and saw my work. He offered to let me apprentice at the shop." She exhaled a soft laugh. "Since no one else was going to hire a homeless fourteen-year-old, I decided taking a chance on Oz was better than panhandling tourists."

Mathias listened, moved that she had opened up this small bit of her past to him. He still didn't know where she'd been before arriving in London at such a tender age, nor did he know the circumstances behind why she'd run...or from whom. He didn't know her full name. Hell, he wasn't at all convinced that Nova was even her true first name.

All things he was patient to wait for, answers he realized he didn't need to have at all, in order to care for her the way he did already.

He kissed her again, then reached for the hem of her black tank top and slowly drew it up, over her head.

Below the phoenix tattoo with its spread wings and scarlet Breedmate mark at its heart, Nova's torso was a clear canvas of milky, unblemished skin. Her small breasts were perfect little globes, capped with sweet pink nipples just begging to be tasted. He could hardly wait, but he had to—at least, until he was sure Nova was ready for all he craved of her.

"You're beautiful, with and without the ink," he murmured, his voice rasping, thick with want. He took her right hand in his, looked down at the modified tattoo that was no doubt a constant reminder of her past, of all she fought so fiercely to leave behind. "You're safe with me. I promise you that."

She nodded, but it was a faint acknowledgment. Although Nova had proven herself unbreakable in escaping whatever horrors she'd endured, there was a fragility in her eyes as she watched him explore her body with his gaze and his touch.

"You can trust me," he said, then bent

down and kissed her, slowly, deeply.

It was too much—that fresh meeting of their mouths after he was already taut with desire for her. Mathias growled low in the back of his throat as his tongue tangled with hers, their lips wet and hot, their slow kiss turning fevered and unstoppable.

He needed to feel her against him.

He needed to be inside her, his impatience held back on the thinnest of tethers.

But her pleasure meant more to him in that moment.

He pulled his mouth away from hers on a snarl. "Lie back."

She did as he asked, and when she was settled flat on the bed, he prowled onto the mattress with her, straddling her knees. He soaked her in with his gaze, the coal-bright glow of his Breed irises bathing her skin in soft amber.

Slowly, he tugged down her loose black sweat pants, baring the tops of her hip bones and the subtle dip of her slender abdomen. Mathias's mouth watered as he glimpsed the lace edges of her panties—bright pink, silky, surprisingly girly.

"Always the unexpected with you," he remarked, grinning through his teeth and fangs.

She smiled up at him. "I'd hate to be boring."

"I don't think you ever have to worry about that."

He drew her pants all the way off and dropped them to the floor. Nova's lean legs were as clear as her torso, just smooth skin that tempted Mathias's hands. He stroked the length of her limbs, slowing as he reached the apex of her thighs. Heat met his fingers as he toyed with the lacy scrap of fabric that covered her sex.

He could smell the sweetness of her arousal, could feel the wet warmth of her bloom even more as he caressed her mound. Unable to resist, he followed his touch with his mouth, bending over her and nuzzling his face against the triangle of pink satin.

Nova gasped, shuddering at the contact. She reached for his head, but instead of pulling him away from her, she held on, her fingers spearing into his hair. Mathias groaned, knowing he was lost now.

He caught her panties between his teeth and drew them down, away from the trimmed patch of tight curls. Then he chuckled, having just discovered something else he hadn't been expecting about his raven-haired beauty. He arched a brow at her. "Blonde?"

She shrugged, shot him a playful smirk. "You never asked."

He grinned back at her, but he wasn't about

to let her have the last laugh. As payback, he dived into that tempting little thatch with his lips and tongue, wringing a startled cry out of her as he sought—and found—the bundle of nerves nestled between her folds.

He suckled her, kissing her as passionately and deeply here as he'd kissed her mouth a few moments ago. He didn't let up until she was writhing under him, her hands twisting in the sheets as her body arched against his lips and tongue.

"Oh, God," she gasped, panting as he took her even higher. "Oh, fuck...Mathias..."

He glanced up as her orgasm rolled through her. She watched him too, her eyes locked on his as her pleasure crested, overflowed.

Mathias held her gaze, giving her a silent promise that this was only the beginning of what he intended to show her.

He wanted to make up for all of the abuses she had suffered at the hands of another, even if it took the rest of his life to help her forget.

Hell, watching her surrender so openly to him now, there was a part of him ready to give her an eternity.

If he had anything to say about it, this moment was already the start.

"Mathias," she murmured, breathless from the aftershocks of her climax. "I don't want this feeling to stop. Not yet..."

"No," he growled. "Not yet."

Stripped out of his clothing and boots, he then knelt beside her, growing hungrier, impossibly harder, as she drank in his nakedness with passion-drunk, heavy-lidded eyes.

His pulse hammered in his ears, in his temples, his blood running like molten lava in his veins from the intensity of his need for this woman. His *glyphs* surged with heat, color flooding their swirling, arcing patterns on his chest and shoulders and biceps.

His fangs pressed against his tongue, razor-sharp tips fully extended, and he knew that Nova was seeing him at his most inhuman—in his savage, predator's form.

She didn't flinch.

She didn't tremble.

She reached for him. *"Mathias..."*

There was nothing more she needed to do or say.

He kissed her, unhurried, and positioned himself between her parted thighs. Her cleft was slick and hot against his shaft as guided himself to her. He couldn't stop now. His desire for her swamped all of his senses.

He pulled his hips back until he was seated at the core of her ready body.

Then he drove home, inch by delicious inch, into the sweetest, hottest pleasure he'd ever known.

~ ~ ~

He filled her more deeply than she thought possible, cleaving her core with so much heat and strength and passion that she could hardly draw her breath. The sensation overwhelmed her, stunned her.

Obliterated every thought she'd ever had for what it meant to be at the mercy of a man's carnal needs.

Nova clung to Mathias as he rocked into her with unbridled force.

Her body was still pliant from its release, nerve endings still thrumming from the pleasure he'd given her with his lips and tongue and touch.

She felt that release winding up again as he crashed against her, the friction of his cock moving inside her swiftly becoming more than she could bear.

On a cry, she shattered. Felt herself splintering apart into tiny pieces.

Without warning, sudden tears filled her eyes. Burned the back of her throat.

Mathias went stock-still above her, halting in mid-thrust. His breath sawed out of him, and the curse he swore was abrupt, dread-filled. "You're crying."

She gave a feeble shake of her head, struggling to find her voice. "I just...I thought it would be different," she choked out. "I thought I could handle it..."

"Ah, shit. God damn it." Every muscle in his body had ceased moving now. His scowl deepened. He started to withdraw from her. "Nova, I'm sorry—"

"No." She clutched his shoulders and swallowed back the raw lump that was blocking her voice. When he continued to shift his weight off her, she wrapped her legs around the backs of his thighs to hold him in place. "No, Mathias. That's not what I mean. I'm not crying because you did anything wrong. It's because this feels so incredible. *You* feel incredible inside me. I wasn't prepared for this—for how we'd feel together. I didn't expect it."

In his silence, he stared at her, unmoving. His fiery gaze warmed her face with its heat. "You feel all right, then?"

"More than all right," she assured him. "I feel...alive. With you inside me like this, I feel whole. For the first time, Mathias, I feel like the rest is really behind me. You've given me that."

He swore again, something low and reverent. Then he kissed her with more tenderness, more aching pleasure, than her heart seemed able to contain.

When he finally broke the contact, he was

grinning, fangs glinting.

She frowned up at him. "What's so funny?"

"Nothing," he murmured, giving his hips a meaningful grind against hers. "I just think it could be amusing, doing other things you'll enjoy but might not expect. Finding ways to keep you guessing, for a change."

He was still moving within her, still hard. Getting harder, in fact.

Nova caressed his face, his handsome, otherworldly face. She wondered how long it would take for her to tire of looking at him.

Longer than she dared imagine.

A lifetime and then some.

She held on as he found his tempo once more. Sighed with pleasure as his rising rhythm steered her toward the edges of another crest of sensation. Closing her eyes, she let him take her there, rode with him as his large body began to go rigid and tense, his hips pumping harder now, furious and deep.

She cried out his name. Heard him mutter hers on a coarse shout beside her ear in that next instant, as heat exploded within her and he shook with the force of his orgasm.

Nova's heart was pounding like thunder in her ears.

Then she heard the rumble again—a rapid drumming, urgent and unsteady. Coming from the other room.

Mathias heard it too, no doubt before she had. He reared back abruptly.

"Nova." Eddie's voice sounded oddly thin outside the apartment door.

"Something's wrong." Mathias said it before she could voice her concern. His face was grim, nostrils flaring. "There is blood."

"Oh, God." Alarm jolted her off the bed. She hurried back into her tank and sweat pants and was racing out to the living area in the next instant. She yanked open the door and shock hit her like a punch to the gut. "Eddie...oh, my God!"

The boy was white as a ghost, his eyes dilated with shock. Blood stained the front of his T-shirt and jeans. A lot of blood.

Nova grabbed him and hugged him close. She felt for injuries, but he seemed unharmed. Her hands came away sticky and red. "What happened to you? Where's Ozzy?"

"In the shop," he murmured, his voice thready. "I couldn't do anything, Nova. He told me to hide. I wanted to help him, but he wouldn't let me."

Panic seized her. "Ozzy?" she shouted into the silence of the building.

Mathias stood behind her now, bare-chested, dressed only in his black pants. Nova swung her gaze up at him, a raw sob hitching in her throat.

"Oh, God. What the hell is going on? Oz!"

She lunged past Eddie, only to be halted when Mathias took hold of her arm. "Nova, stay here. Let me—"

She wrenched loose on a miserable cry and bolted for the stairs leading down to the studio.

CHAPTER 8

C

"Ozzy...oh, no. No!"

Nova found him in the empty tattoo shop, lying in a pool of blood near his station. Dropped in a ragdoll sprawl on his back, his body was motionless, his eyes frozen wide. His throat was gashed open, hideously savaged.

"Oz!" she cried, standing barefoot at the edge of the blood pool, her hands covering her mouth as a howl of anguish tore out of her. "No, Ozzy. No..."

"I was sweeping the back room after Ozzy finished with a client, when I heard a man come into the shop," Eddie murmured from behind her at the bottom of the stairs. "He was looking for someone. Looking for you, Nova."

Confusion jabbed through her grief as she

stared down at the savagery done to her beloved mentor. "Looking for me? Are you sure?"

"He didn't seem to know your name," Eddie went on, "but the man knew what you looked like. He told Ozzy, asked if he knew you. The man said it was important that he find you. He said you were in trouble."

She frowned, trying to make sense of the horror in front of her. Even in her state of numb shock, she could scent the lie in what the attacker told Ozzy. "Did you see who it was, Eddie?"

"No. He was wearing dark clothes, had a hooded jacket on. I only saw him from the side, as he walked over to Ozzy's station." Eddie released a shuddering breath. "He was big, Nova. He sounded mean, angry. I could tell Ozzy was scared of him too."

She closed her eyes, fear pouring into her veins. "Was he human?"

"I don't know," Eddie said. "I tried to look, but I couldn't see his face. The man didn't see me standing in the back room. I wanted to tell him to leave Ozzy alone, but Oz motioned for me to stay put. He mouthed for me not to say anything, to hide..." The boy choked on a sob. "So, I did. I crawled into a cabinet and I hid, Nova. And then I heard the man hurting Oz..."

She glanced behind her at Eddie, and saw

Mathias, now arrived at the bottom of the stairs.

"You did the right thing," he told the kid, who had dissolved into wracking tears. "If you hadn't done what Ozzy told you, both of you would be dead now, Eddie."

The boy looked up at him. "You were here last night. Were you upstairs with Nova just now?"

Mathias gave a slight nod. His gaze was solemn, grave. And in the pools of pale green that met Nova's eyes now, she saw the crackle of amber sparks. She saw the tips of his fangs too, and the flush of color that was slowly seeping into the *dermaglyphs* on his bare chest.

The sight of so much spilled, fresh blood could not have been easy for him. His Breed nature must have been clawing at him, yet Mathias held his vampire side at bay with remarkable control. For Eddie's sake, no doubt. Maybe for her sake too.

Nova's own jagged sob scraped in her throat as she looked down at Ozzy again.

She didn't hear Mathias move up behind her.

She didn't know he was close enough to touch her, until his warm palm settled lightly, tenderly, on her shoulder. "Nova—"

"Don't." She shrank away from his comfort. The idea that she had been mindless with passion, crying out in pleasure with Mathias while Ozzy was being attacked and murdered right under them was a pain she could hardly bear. She stared at Mathias in abject misery, guilt and grief shredding her from the inside. Her voice came out flat, forbidding. "Don't touch me."

He frowned, letting his hand fall to his side. "Eddie, did the man say anything else to Ozzy?"

"No. He wanted to know where to find Nova. Ozzy wouldn't tell him, and then the man got really mad." Eddie sniffled. "Is the man going to hurt Nova next?"

"No," Mathias answered sternly, swiftly. "I'll never allow that to happen. I won't let anything bad happen to you either, Eddie. But the two of you can't stay here now. I'm going to call in some people who can help me look after Ozzy, then I'm going to bring you both someplace safe with me."

He reached for Nova as he said it. She couldn't curb her knee-jerk reaction, the jolt of denial and grief that sliced into her at the thought of going anywhere without Oz.

"I'm not leaving him." She pulled out of Mathias's reach. Cold, thickening blood was slippery under the bare soles of her feet as she moved closer to Ozzy's body. "I need to know what happened. I need to know who did this."

She dropped down on her knees beside him.

Mathias saw what she was about to do. He scowled, started to shake his head. "Nova, don't—"

His caution was a distant echo in her ears as she reached out and took hold of Ozzy's lifeless hand.

The final moments of his life played out behind her closed eyelids, just as Eddie had described them. The immense man in dark clothing, his face all but obscured by the hood of his black jacket. The demands he made of Ozzy, his low voice deadly with menace.

Then Ozzy's courageous, foolish, effort to protect her. To lie for her, even when he knew it would likely cost him his life.

Nova saw the sharp blade coming up from behind Oz as the man overpowered him. Sliced deep into his throat. Let him drop to the floor in a convulsing, sputtering heap, Ozzy's last conscious memory the swift, retreating form of his killer as the assailant vanished from the shop with inhuman speed and agility.

Because he hadn't been human.

"He was Breed," Nova murmured, as the connection to Ozzy's death faded from her grasp. "The man who killed him...he was Breed."

~ ~ ~

Twenty minutes later, fully dressed and grim with scarcely contained menace, Mathias waited for his backup to arrive. He'd called his squad of warriors in from chasing their tails looking for Rogues down in Lambeth to assist him with a real problem. An immediate one that he meant to deal with using all of the manpower and resources in his reach. That included his friend Sloane, who'd offered to put a full taskforce on the case when Mathias spoke with the JUSTIS officer a short while ago.

Hell, if Mathias had to call in favors from every Order commander in the United States and abroad to shake out his quarry, he damned well would.

The man who killed Ozzy, and was very likely still on the hunt for Nova, was going to pay.

With his lifeblood, if Mathias got to him first.

Seeing Nova's pain—Eddie's too—there was nothing that would satisfy Mathias more than to be the one to personally slay the son of a bitch.

That the killer could be Breed only made it more crucial that they find him. Bad enough to know there were human thugs like Doyle and his scarab-marked colleagues skulking around London with the potential to do harm to Nova.

To think she could be in the crosshairs of a predator with the Breed's deadly appetites and skills?

Mathias snarled through his fangs, prowling the studio like a caged animal as he waited for Thane and Deacon to arrive. The third member of the patrol, Callahan, would be hoofing it across town to meet them at the shop. Thane informed Mathias that the impulsive young warrior had gone off to find a blood Host and feed, after the team's Rogue hunt had proven a bust.

As for JUSTIS, Sloane had been tied up on another investigation, but expected he could be there with his unit within the hour.

In the meantime, the waiting was making Mathias crazy.

The sense of helplessness wasn't something he was accustomed to, but that feeling had less to do with the anticipated reconnoiter with his team and JUSTIS than it did with Nova.

After using her ability on Ozzy, she'd come away viciously nauseated, barely making it to the restroom in the back of the shop before she lost her stomach.

She'd been in the back room with Eddie ever since, a closed door standing as a barrier between them and Mathias in the studio.

That door wasn't the only obstacle between Nova and him now.

She didn't want to be near him.

She didn't want his comfort or his concern.

She didn't want anything from him.

And not that he could blame her. He'd been sick with himself too, cursing himself for the recklessness that had not only cost Ozzy's life tonight, but had left Nova in the crosshairs of a killer. One who might be closing in on her even now.

As much as Mathias hated that she'd used her ESP gift to try to identify Ozzy's murderer, he had to admit he'd been hoping the vision would have given him something useful to go on in his pursuit of the bastard.

He hadn't wanted Nova to do it. He tried to stop her, knowing what that horrible glimpse would cost her. The experience of Ozzy's death would be one she'd have to carry with her forever.

She'd already known enough pain and ugliness in her life. Mathias wanted to shield her from any more. Difficult to do, when she wasn't even speaking to him now.

He cursed and sent his fist into the nearest wall.

He'd failed her tonight.

If he hadn't been so caught up in his enjoyment of Nova's body, of her sweet but fiery passion, maybe he would have heard the confrontation taking place in the shop two floors down. Maybe he would have scented the blood in the air before Eddie came to the door. Maybe he could have stopped Ozzy's killing and spared Nova the grief that was tearing her apart now.

Maybe...

Fuck. All he had was maybes when it came to that woman.

His woman.

To his astonishment, he realized he couldn't think of Nova in any other way.

He was about to turn around and tell her when the Order's black Range Rover rolled up to the curb outside the tattoo shop. As Thane and Deacon jumped out, Sloane blazed in behind them in an unmarked vehicle with its dashboard LED flashing, another JUSTIS unit pulling up behind him. Not a few moments later, Callahan emerged from somewhere in the darkness and came jogging up to the shop.

Mathias walked out to greet the arriving warriors and his friend from JUSTIS.

His talk with Nova would have to wait.

Right now, he had a killer to hunt down and destroy.

~ ~ ~

Nova had done her best to clean up Eddie and herself in the shop's small restroom.

There wasn't enough water in London to wash out all of the blood that stained the shell-shocked kid's shirt and trembling hands. She'd tried to scrub it off her too, from her fingers and bare feet, the knees of her dark sweats gore-soaked from when she'd knelt down beside Ozzy to relive his last moments of life.

The sink had run red down the drain for fifteen minutes straight before she'd finally given up. Nothing to do for their clothes but burn them.

She dropped Eddie's ruined T-shirt in the restroom trash bin and gave him a tender look. "You okay?"

He nodded weakly, then shook his head. His eyes were still puffy and moist from his tears. His mouth quivered as he spoke. "What are we gonna do, Nova?"

She offered him a smile, but it felt wobbly and uncertain on her lips. "We'll figure it out."

The same words Mathias had spoken to her earlier that night, when she'd finally admitted to him that she didn't have her shit together at all, that she was scared.

She was still scared, even more so now. Not only because Ozzy was gone, and she didn't know what her life was going to be like without the old man being part of it, but because she had somehow let another man into her life.

Into her heart.

Mathias.

How had she been so careless as to let her guard down with him, after a lifetime of keeping herself safely closed off, her wants and desires sealed up behind steep, unbreachable tower walls?

How had he managed to crash the gate, when she'd barely had time to prepare for the battle?

As much as Nova wanted to blame herself—blame him—for Ozzy's suffering tonight while they'd been so blissfully, selfishly unaware, there was another part of her that wanted nothing more than to open the door and run to Mathias. For his comfort, for his strength.

And yes, for his love.

She needed all of those things from him, and she wasn't afraid to admit, if only to herself.

Looking at Eddie, standing there half-dressed, his scrawny chest and shoulders shuddering under the weight of his shock and fear, Nova knew that she also needed Mathias's protection. For the kid.

For herself as well.

Amid all of the horror and anguish tonight over the loss of Ozzy, she couldn't afford to forget that there was a killer searching for her.

A savage Breed male who'd shown very clearly that he wasn't going to let anyone get in his way of finding her.

Not even an innocent boy.

So much the worse, if Ozzy's killer knew that Eddie had been nearby the whole time, close enough to hear him, and to know what he'd done to Oz.

What if the killer decided to come back to the shop?

What if he was somewhere outside, watching, waiting for a chance to make another move?

What if it was someone sent by her father—someone worse than Doyle or his other human thugs?

Each possibility seemed more awful than the next. The one thing she was certain of, was that the shop was no place for Eddie to be right now. Mathias had offered to take them somewhere safe tonight. Maybe she should let him.

She wrapped her arm around Eddie. "Let's go talk to Mathias, okay?"

The boy nodded, and she started to guide him toward the closed door leading out to the studio.

Started to, but stopped.

Mathias was no longer alone in the shop.

And as the din of male voices grew louder out there—Mathias's colleagues from the Order and JUSTIS, all now arrived—Nova's heart froze in her breast.

A glance over at Eddie confirmed her dread.

His freckled face had gone ghostly white, his eyes wide with fear.

"You hear him too?" she whispered.

Eddie nodded, silent.

The voice Nova heard when she relived Ozzy's death. The voice that had terrified Eddie from inside the cabinet where he'd hid during the murder.

The man it belonged to was in the other room with Mathias now.

He had to be warned. But how could she do it, without exposing herself and Eddie to Ozzy's murderer at the same time?

Nova pushed the boy back, away from the door. Then she gently, soundlessly, opened it just the tiniest crack. Her heart lurched, dread like ice in her chest.

Mathias was conversing in low, serious tones with the other men. He was obviously friendly with them all.

Friends with them all.

Including the one whose voice went through Nova as sharp as the blade that had slashed Ozzy's throat.

That man and a few others now broke away from the others with Mathias and started heading for the back room.

Were there more than just the one involved?

Could Mathias possibly know?

And then, a sickening, worrisome thought: Is that why he had tried to stop her from touching Ozzy? Because he was afraid of what she'd see through Ozzy's eyes?

She didn't want to think it.

She wanted to believe her trust in him was well-placed, that it was real.

But Mathias was still approaching, leading Ozzy's killer right to her.

No. Oh, God...no.

She couldn't let him see her. She couldn't let him get near Eddie.

Nova retreated from the door.

"Come on," she whispered, barely making a sound. "We have to get out of here. Now."

CHAPTER 9

Mathias was more impatient than anyone to begin the hunt for Ozzy's killer, but before he could even think about hitting the street with his team and the JUSTIS officers who'd arrived to assist, he had to make sure Nova and Eddie were safe.

He'd tasked Callahan with taking them back to the Order's command center in the heart of London. Although it was rare—almost unheard of—that civilians were permitted into Order compounds, Mathias was willing to bend that rule for Nova.

If he had anything to say about it, she wasn't going to be merely a civilian for long, anyway. He wanted her in his life. Hell, he wanted her as his mate, if she'd have him.

The Rover was still idling at the curb. All

Mathias needed to do was convince Nova that she needed to trust him, that she needed to do what he asked for once and let him take care of her.

He walked to the back room with Callahan and a few other men. Mathias knocked on the door at the same time he started to open it. "Nova, I've made arrangements for you and Eddie at—"

She was gone.

The back room was vacant. The rear door letting out onto the alleyway behind the shop was partially ajar, admitting a thin draft of night air inside.

Nova had left, taking Eddie with her. The reality of it raked over Mathias with cold claws.

Fuck. She was out there on her own right now, while Ozzy's killer was still very much at large.

She had to be aware of that danger. And yet she'd chosen that risk over staying another minute under Mathias's watch.

"Damn it, Nova." He turned to the three warriors behind him, an odd chill blooming behind his sternum. "She won't be coming back."

"Where do you think she went?" Callahan asked.

Mathias lifted his shoulder. "I don't know. She could be anywhere in the city."

"If she's on foot, she can't be far," Deacon said.

Thane nodded, his black brows knit together over dark eyes. "You want us to go after her, Commander?"

"No," Mathias said after a moment, the word heavy on his tongue.

Every particle of his being pounded with the need to bring her back to him. But if he sent warriors after her now, it would only make her run farther.

Nova was a smart woman and a proven survivor. He had to trust she'd find a way to keep herself and Eddie safe.

The best thing he could do for her was make damned sure the Breed bastard who killed Ozzy wasn't permitted to breathe for much longer tonight.

Sloane stood behind Deacon and Callahan at the door. The JUSTIS officer shot Mathias a disapproving look. "You've got a body lying in a lake of blood out there, a missing woman and kid, and no one here to explain what happened tonight except you, my friend. I think you'd better tell us what's going on."

He had filled them all in briefly when he'd called them to the shop, alerting them to the murder and the fact that the killer had been looking for a woman who worked there. It hadn't seemed the best time to mention that he'd been at the scene when the assault took place, let alone that he'd been in an upstairs apartment making love to the very woman the attacker had come in to find.

Although Sloane had demanded the answers, Mathias spoke to his team. "I met Nova here at the shop two nights ago, during our search for the tattoo artist who'd left the unfinished work on the last guy fished out of the Thames."

"A lucky break," Deacon remarked. "We searched a dozen shops and came up empty."

"Yeah, well," Mathias hedged. "As soon as I got near Ozzy's shop, I sensed something was off. I could tell there'd been an altercation here, a pretty bad one. It made me curious, so I stopped in, asked a few questions."

"What did you find out?" Thane asked.

"That our dead scarab had, indeed, been in the shop. He came in the night before, and Nova was the one who did the tattoo."

"But she didn't finish it," Callahan said.

"No. The guy was drunk, belligerent. There were words exchanged, then threats. Things turned ugly, and Ozzy killed him to protect Nova. They dumped the body in the river."

"Jesus Christ," Sloane muttered.

Mathias went on, holding his old friend's rightfully indignant look. Sloane wasn't going to like anything else he would hear now either. "I realized there were things she wasn't telling me. I suspected some kind of connection between her and the man who came into the shop...and I was right. She knew him. She didn't know the others in the morgue, but she was scared enough to go there and find out what she could about them."

Now, Sloane's hissed curse was even more profane. "You lied to me earlier today, Rowan. You acted like you had no goddamned idea who woman in the morgue video was. Yet all along you knew."

"I knew," he admitted soberly. "I'm telling you now, lying to my friends—to my teammates—goes against everything I am. But when it comes to this woman, when it comes to Nova..."

"You care for her," Thane said.

Mathias nodded. He glanced to Sloane. "When you told me she had been at the morgue to see the other dead men, I didn't know how deeply she might be involved in any of this. I didn't know if she had been part of the other killings too. I didn't know if she'd been lying to me about what she knew. I only knew I had to give her the chance to tell me first. So, as soon as the sun set, I came here to talk with her."

"You've been here all night?" Callahan piped up. "You were here while the killing took place?"

"I was upstairs, in Nova's apartment with her." He didn't have to elaborate on what he was doing up there. The looks he was getting from all four men said they understood plainly enough. "I didn't know about the attack until after it was over. The boy, Eddie, was in the shop when the killer arrived. Eddie hid back there, in the storage room. He ran upstairs to Nova's afterward, in a state of shock."

"He didn't see who did it?" Deacon asked.

"No, but Nova did." At the round of confused glances that fixed on him, Mathias explained. "She's a Breedmate. Her gift lets her see the final moments of someone's life when she touches them. When she touched Ozzy, she saw a Breed male in a hooded jacket. She saw this male slash open her friend's throat."

Mathias now looked to Sloane. "That's what Nova was doing at the morgue this morning, when she touched the dead men with the scarab tattoos. She saw that there was some kind of meeting taking place between those men and a group of Russians. The thug who confronted her here in Ozzy's shop the other night was there too. She saw him execute his own men."

Sloane stared at him, raked a hand over his head. "For fuck's sake, Rowan. When were you going to divulge all of this intel? Things between our two organizations are touchy enough without the commander of the Order's operation in London willfully interfering in an open JUSTIS investigation. Withholding information, diverting resources, fucking a person of interest—"

Mathias growled at that last charge, even though he was guilty of everything Sloane pointed out. "I want this thing sewn up as much as anyone else—more than anyone, I'd say. But Nova is my responsibility. I don't want anyone questioning her, or pointing one damned finger at her without coming to me first—"

Sloane studied him through narrowed blue eyes. "Have you drunk from this female? Have you blood-bonded to her?" When Mathias shook his head in denial, Sloane scoffed. "No, but you want to."

He wasn't going to refute that. He couldn't.

While he'd lived a very long life taking his sustenance from willing human females— women who provided sex and nourishment and little more—he'd had no appetite for basic Homo sapiens blood anymore.

Not since he'd first laid eyes on an ink-covered, metal-studded, thoroughly unconventional beauty named Nova.

If he drank from her, a Breedmate, one sip would mean forever.

A concept Mathias was more than willing to explore with her. If she'd have him, and if he managed to find her before the danger on her heels came any closer than it already had.

"It doesn't matter what I want right now," he told Sloane and his team from the Order. "I just need to make sure Nova and the boy are safe, and that starts by finding the murdering bastard who was here in this shop earlier tonight."

With his warriors dispatched to split up and hit the surrounding area streets on foot, and the JUSTIS unit augmenting the search by vehicle, Mathias then turned to Sloane. "The killer didn't come here looking for Nova by accident. He must've had access to the video from the morgue. I know you don't have a lot of reason to do me any favors right now—"

"No, I don't," the JUSTIS officer grumbled. "But lucky for you, I don't hold a grudge. You want a list of all the eyes that saw that video?"

"And anyone who handled the reports of the dead scarabs," Mathias added, quirking a brow when Sloane shot him an arch look. "I appreciate it."

The Breed male grunted. "I'll go make a few calls. I'll alert the coroner's office to the situation too."

Mathias cuffed his old friend on the shoulder and murmured his thanks as Sloane stepped outside. Alone in Ozzy's shop, the blood coagulated under the sheet-covered body, and far less potent to his Breed senses, Mathias took a moment to consider everything that had happened that night.

His concern for Nova's safety, and the need to know that he hadn't lost her completely, had his emotions combating his warrior instincts most of the time following Ozzy's murder. And now that he was resolved, a plan being put into place, he realized that something was gnawing at the edges of his mind.

He couldn't shake the feeling that he was missing something crucial.

The pieces weren't quite fitting together for him, and he kept coming back to the fact that something just didn't feel right.

Sloane walked back inside, slipping his comm unit back into his pocket. "Since you're begging favors from JUSTIS tonight, you want me to put an alert out on your female? Ordinarily, a missing persons call doesn't go out until twenty-four hours pass, but I see nothing wrong in bending the rules for a friend."

"No, but thanks," he replied, those prickly instincts still nagging him.

As much as he appreciated Sloane's offer of support, he preferred to keep all eyes focused on finding the killer. And there was a part of him that wouldn't trust anyone where Nova was concerned.

He thought back to what she'd told him

about the things she saw when she touched the dead scarabs in the morgue. "Nova said there was someone else on the dock that night," he murmured, thinking out loud. "Someone who shot and killed one of the Russians, maybe more than one."

Sloane grunted. "That's odd. The only thing we pulled out of the river so far are dead scarabs. Not a single Russian among them."

"She seemed pretty certain that's what she saw," Mathias said. "Which means we've got another killer out there."

"Maybe that's the guy we need to be looking for tonight," Sloane suggested. "Was she able to ID anything useful about the guy who shot the Russians?"

"She didn't say."

"But she was sure it wasn't Doyle?"

Every tendon in Mathias's body went as tight as a bowstring. His veins started to pound. "Yes, she was sure..."

He glanced at Sloane, who had now gone equally still, staring back at him.

"I never told you his name," Mathias said.

At first, he thought Sloane was going to deny it. But then the big Breed male cocked his head slightly, a wry smile lifting one corner of his mouth. "No. I guess you didn't."

Mathias felt sucker-punched. He looked at his old friend in sickened disbelief. "You did this tonight? You would've killed her too?"

"It wasn't about the old man or the girl. They had nothing to do with any of this." Sloane's eyes took on a flinty edge. "If you want to blame someone, blame that drunken idiot, Doyle. He's the one who put the target on their backs. He had no damned business letting himself be seen anywhere people might know him. So, he goes off and gets a tattoo? Fucking humans."

Mathias dismissed the rant with a snarl. "Tell me what's going on, Sloane. You and Doyle. It was you with him that night at the docks? What were you two doing? What kind of deal were you trying to make that night?"

He gave a slow shake of his head. "My only hand in the deal was to make sure things went smoothly, and that no one got nosy that night."

"You and Doyle," Mathias pressed. "You killed all of those people in cold blood?"

"They were scum, all of them. Especially Doyle. I would've killed him soon enough too, but your female and the old man here did the job for me."

"Why? Are you a scarab too?"

"Fuck no," Sloane spat out. "My only affiliation is to myself."

"Then how'd you get mixed up in all of this?"

Sloane grinned. "I got paid, friend. I got

paid very fucking well to make sure a package reached its destination, and that there were no loose ends." He chuckled. "Guess I'm the last one."

"What about Nova?" Mathias said. "Is anyone else after her?"

"No one ever was. I don't know what her connection was to Doyle or his associates outside London, and I don't care." He shrugged. "Far as I'm concerned, she was just in the wrong place at the wrong time."

Mathias was relieved to hear it, but still cognizant of the fact that Nova's past would need to be dealt with at some point. When she was ready. And he meant to be at her side when that day came.

"I have to take you in, Gavin."

He stared, expressionless. "We both know that's not gonna happen."

Slowly, he turned around as if he meant to stroll out of the shop.

Mathias pulled his gun from its holster on his weapons belt. He cocked the 9mm pistol. "Sloane, stop."

He paused, but didn't turn around. His arms hung loosely at his sides. "You gonna put a bullet in my back?"

Mathias cursed through gritted teeth. "I'd rather not. But you're not walking out that door."

"Okay," Sloane said after a moment. "I'll make it easy on you."

He pivoted suddenly, and Mathias saw that he was holding his own gun. It exploded an instant later, and a fireball of pain opened up in Mathias's gut.

He fired back.

His bullet hit his old friend between the eyes.

Sloane hit the floor.

Mathias staggered down to one knee, blood pouring out of him.

CHAPTER 10

Mathias walked into the war room of the Order's London command center that next morning, a bandage wrapped around his bare midsection. His pain was mild, but the gunshot wound that perforated several internal organs was going to take a few more hours to heal.

He hadn't been happy to be dragged to headquarters by Thane and his other men after he called them back to Ozzy's shop. He'd wanted to go looking for Nova last night. Turn the city inside-out in order to find her and tell her that Ozzy's killer was dead and she had no reason to be afraid.

But dawn had been coming fast, and the bullet Gavin Sloane had fired through him had grounded Mathias on base for the rest of the night instead.

The Order's report overnight of Gavin Sloane's death in the line of duty had been met with shock by his colleagues at JUSTIS. The fact that the long-time law enforcement officer had been corrupt, on the take from a troubling underworld organization with ties and motives not yet determined, had been a detail Lucan Thorne had decided to omit from any official filings.

Documents had been pulled, photographs and video destroyed, data obliterated. And, where necessary, human minds had been scrubbed of any and all recollection to the contrary of what Mathias's official statement read.

For all anyone knew outside the Order, Sloane had stumbled upon the scene of a homicide at a Southwark tattoo shop, apparently surprising a pair of perpetrators—one who had a knife, the other a gun. Unfortunately for Sloane, Mathias and his patrol team from the Order discovered the crime too late to save the respected Breed officer, who had been killed with a lucky shot to the head, the criminals having fled the scene.

Never to be seen or heard from again, of course.

As for Mathias and his team, they were already looking into another unusual string of killings.

It seemed someone had begun quietly targeting London's banking community. Three high-ranking finance executives had been found dead in their homes in the past handful of days—one victim human, the other two Breed. JUSTIS was under immediate and great pressure to make the murders stop before the public found out and began to panic.

Mathias understood the urgency, but his mind was on another unresolved matter of great concern.

He had to see Nova again.

He had to let her know she was safe.

And that she would always be safe, so long as he had breath in his body and blood running through his eternal veins.

He just needed to find her first.

"Nice ink," Callahan said, strolling into the room to where Mathias sat with a computer tablet, reviewing the intel from the recent murders. The young warrior sat down next to Mathias at the workstation, studying the sword tattoo on his back. "Think your lady will do one for me?"

"I don't know," Mathias answered. "What would you want?"

The warrior shrugged. "Something badass, like the one you have."

"No way," he said. "That one belongs all to

me."

And so does the woman who created it.

"What about the one you're drawing on that report, then?"

"Hmm?" Mathias glanced down to where he'd been idly toying with the stylus on the tablet. He didn't have a fraction of Nova's talent, but he recognized the symbol immediately.

The rose window from the ruins of Winchester Palace.

One of Nova's many tattoos.

One that meant something very important to her.

And that was where he would start looking for her as soon as night fell.

~ ~ ~

Nova tucked Eddie into the thin cot in the basement of the cathedral. The poor kid was exhausted. She was too. She sat on the edge of the mattress and smoothed his hair off his drowsy face.

"How long do we have to stay here?" he asked her, his words slurred from the sleep that was already pulling him under.

"I don't know," she answered. "For a while. Until I find us someplace better."

He nodded sleepily. "Okay. Just don't leave

me."

"Never," she whispered, realizing only now that she had just stepped into Ozzy's shoes. They wouldn't be easy to fill. But she would do her best. She would find a way to give Eddie the same security and support that Oz had given her all those years ago.

God, she missed him already.

Would always miss him.

And she missed Mathias too, although that was a pain she didn't have to accept.

She could contact him. He'd given her his number. A number she'd tossed in the trash almost the same moment he gave it to her.

Now, she wanted nothing more than to pull that moment back to her. Rewind it. Play it out a different way.

Maybe Ozzy would still be alive.

Maybe she and Mathias would be together.

Maybe she was a fool, losing her heart to someone she'd known only a handful of days.

As Eddie's soft snores drifted up from his pillow, Nova carefully eased herself up off the bed.

It was early, just past sundown. She was restless, twitchy, even though she hadn't slept more than a few minutes last night.

She glanced around at the dozens of other similar cots, occupied by men and women and children, a community of all ages and descriptions. She was homeless again. Faced with the decision to either run some more or hide.

She needed space to think. Time to heal after Ozzy's death and all of the awful things that had surrounded it.

And she needed to feel Mathias's arms around her, with a desperation she could hardly reconcile.

She'd fallen in love with him.

She didn't know how, didn't care why.

She only knew that she needed him.

And right now, all she wanted to do was walk out into the night air and scream Mathias's name.

Quietly, she left the basement shelter and walked up the stairs to the door leading to the cathedral grounds. She found a wooden bench and sank down onto it. It was a place she'd sat many times before, her private meditation nook in the middle of the bustling city.

Tipping her head back, she looked up, beyond the cathedral towers at the stars and the waning crescent moon. She closed her eyes and remembered the terrified, brutalized little girl who'd come here the first time.

She was back again, scared and hurting, but she was different now. She had a new strength, thanks to Ozzy and the home he had opened to her. Now he was gone, but she was still standing. And he would want her to stand. He wouldn't want her to run.

She didn't want to run, not anymore.

Not from anyone, ever again.

Not even from Mathias, and the feelings he had awakened in her.

"Is this seat taken?"

She dropped her chin, her eyes flying open. "You found me."

"I found you," Mathias said. He sat down next to her on the bench. "Ozzy's killer is dead. You're safe now. I wanted you to know that."

"You...?" she asked, unsure what she needed to know in that moment. The fact that he was there with her was the only thing that really mattered.

"We got him, Nova. And from what we've gathered, it doesn't appear that anyone else knows you're in London. Doyle and the others weren't looking for you. You and Eddie aren't in any danger now."

"Thank you," she murmured. "You came here just to tell me that?"

He nodded. "Are you...all right?"

"I miss Oz," she admitted. "I'll always miss Oz."

"I know. I'm sorry." He frowned, gave a mild shake of his head. "If there's anything I can do..."

"I'll be fine," she assured him. "Eddie and I

will be fine. We'll figure things out."

Mathias smiled at that, a smile that seemed heavy with regret. "Have you thought about what you'll do...whether you'll go back to Ozzy's place...?"

"I don't want to take Eddie back there," she said, realizing it only now. She hadn't really thought about alternatives, but she knew she'd land on her feet somewhere. "We'll figure things out."

"You already said that," he murmured. He reached out to her, stroked her cheek with a light caress. "Why don't you figure it out while you're staying with me."

Nova frowned. "Staying with you, where?"

"At my place in the city."

"You mean, the Order's headquarters?"

He shrugged. "I'm the commander of the London office. So, technically, the headquarters is my place. You and Eddie would stay with me, in my private quarters in the mansion."

"Mansion," she said. She pictured gleaming marble and elegant furniture. Things she'd known as a child and learned to despise. "I don't know..."

"What don't you know?" The fingers stroking her cheek now wandered into her hair, his warm, strong palm cupping her nape. "Come back with me. There's no point in you and Eddie living here, when I have all the room either of you could ever need."

She shook her head, even as tempted as she was by his offer of comfort and a luxurious place to stay. "It wouldn't be right. I can't trade one temporary shelter for another."

He stared at her, a scowl forming. "No, that wouldn't be right."

She exhaled a heavy, pent-up breath. Letting it out seemed to deflate some of her soul along with it. "I'd rather stop this now, Mathias. I'm not afraid to be on my own, but I don't want to fool myself that accepting your offer won't make it harder for me to leave later."

He nodded soberly. "I agree, that would pose a problem. For both of us. That's why my offer isn't a temporary one."

She gaped at him. "What?"

"I want to take you home with me, Nova. You and Eddie both." He took her face in both hands now, holding her as tenderly as an eggshell. "I want to take you back with me, right now. Where I plan to romance you properly...and thoroughly. You, at any rate. Not the boy."

Nova laughed. "You can't be serious. We hardly know each other."

"We have time. All the time in the world."

"You don't even know my real name."

He smiled, his eyes sparking with challenge and determination. "So, tell me."

"Catriona," she said softly. "Catriona Riordan."

He grunted, as if testing the feel of the name in his mind. "I like it. And I like you. I love you, Nova."

He loved her. Her heart leapt in her breast, a giddy, girly jolt of elation. She'd been so leaden with grief, the joy she felt now was like a sudden burst of sunlight after a heavy storm. "Are you trying to sweep me off my feet or something, Mathias?"

His grin widened. "Like some kind of knight in shining armor, Nova. Yes, that's exactly what I'm trying to do."

She touched his face, his handsome, earnest face. "Well, in that case, I don't mind telling you that I love you too."

"Good answer." He stared into her eyes, his own irises glittering with bright amber sparks. "Now about the rest of my question..."

"The part about spending the rest of my life with you?"

"As my mate," he clarified. "I won't settle for anything less."

"I'm not an easy woman to live with," she warned him. "I'm moody. I'm stubborn. Sometimes I don't play well with others."

"Fortunately for both of us, I enjoy a challenge."

She laughed, then sighed as he pulled her

into his arms and across his lap.

When his mouth found hers and he kissed her, slow and sweet and sensual, she felt all of her fears melt away.

She felt hope, and the promise of a future—and a happiness—she'd long imagined was out of reach.

But nothing was out of her reach now.

Not when her heart was overflowing with love and Mathias was holding her close in his strong arms.

~ * ~

Look for the next novel in the Midnight Breed vampire romance series!

Crave the Night

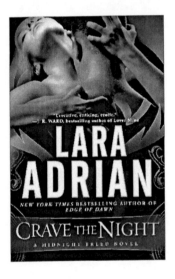

A quest to root out a dangerous enemy of the Order sends ruthless former assassin Nathan from the violent streets of Boston to the glittering world of a Darkhaven beauty he cannot afford to crave.

But seducing Jordana proves a temptation too great to resist, even while his duty to the Order may demand Nathan betray her and all she holds dear.

**On sale August 5, 2014
in hardcover, ebook and unabridged audio book**

ABOUT THE AUTHOR

LARA ADRIAN is a New York Times and #1 internationally best-selling author, with nearly 4 million books in print worldwide and translations licensed to more than 20 countries. Her books regularly appear in the top spots of all the major bestseller lists including the New York Times, USA Today, Publishers Weekly, Indiebound, Amazon.com, Barnes & Noble, etc. Reviewers have called Lara's books "addictively readable" (Chicago Tribune), "extraordinary" (Fresh Fiction), and "one of the best vampire series on the market" (Romantic Times).

Writing as **TINA ST. JOHN**, her historical romances have won numerous awards including the National Readers Choice; Romantic Times Magazine Reviewer's Choice; Booksellers Best; and many others. She was twice named a Finalist in Romance Writers of America's RITA Awards, for Best Historical Romance (White Lion's Lady) and Best Paranormal Romance (Heart of the Hunter). More recently, the German translation of Heart of the Hunter debuted on Der Spiegel bestseller list
.

With an ancestry stretching back to the Mayflower and the court of King Henry VIII, the author lives with her husband in New England.

Visit the author's website and sign up for new release announcements at **www.LaraAdrian.com**.

Thirsty for more Midnight Breed?

Read the complete series!

A Touch of Midnight (prequel novella)
Kiss of Midnight
Kiss of Crimson
Midnight Awakening
Midnight Rising
Veil of Midnight
Ashes of Midnight
Shades of Midnight
Taken by Midnight
Deeper Than Midnight
A Taste of Midnight (ebook novella)
Darker After Midnight
The Midnight Breed Series Companion
Edge of Dawn
Marked by Midnight (novella)
Crave the Night
Tempted by Midnight (novella)

...and more to come!

Upcoming titles from Lara Adrian

<u>Masters of Seduction Series</u>
Merciless: House of Gravori
(in the Masters of Seduction boxed set)

A new paranormal romance series with *New York Times*
bestselling authors Donna Grant, Laura Wright and
Alexandra Ivy

<u>Phoenix Code Series</u>
Cut and Run (Nov 2014)
Hide and Seek (Spring 2015)

A new paranormal romantic suspense series with *New York
Times* bestselling author Tina Folsom

Other books available now

LARA ADRIAN
writing as TINA ST. JOHN

<u>Dragon Chalice Series</u>
Heart of the Hunter
Heart of the Flame
Heart of the Dove

<u>Warrior Trilogy</u>
White Lion's Lady
Black Lion's Bride
Lady of Valor

Standalone Works

Lord of Vengeance

NightDrake (short story)
A Glimpse of Darkness (ebook collaborative novella)

Find Lara Adrian online at:

www.LaraAdrian.com

www.facebook.com/LaraAdrianBooks

www.twitter.com/lara_adrian

www.goodreads.com/lara_adrian

www.pinterest.com/LaraAdrian

www.wattpad.com/user/LaraAdrian